Praise for THE ROMAN MYSTERIES

'From slave traders to criminal masterminds, Flavia Gemina and her fellow sleuths outwit a host of villains in these riveting Roman detective stories. No one is writing crime for children like Caroline Lawrence' *Waterstones*

'Packed with adventure and effortlessly deployed detail culled from Pliny and Juvenal . . . enjoyable entertainment' *The Independent on Sunday*

'. . . a fresh type of historical novel full of drama and fun . . . This series promises many delights to come' *The Times*

'Lively characters, exciting plotlines and the vivid evocation of life in Ancient Rome makes this series hugely popular' *Borders Summer Magazine*

'Lawrence has succeeded in not only vividly and accurately recreating the world of ancient Rome, but has also written some really exciting, child-centred thriller stories . . .' *Northern Echo*

'A great read for kids' *Daily Express*

Also by Caroline Lawrence

THE ROMAN MYSTERIES

The First Roman Mysteries Quiz Book
The Second Roman Mysteries Quiz Book
Trimalchio's Feast and Other Mini-Mysteries
The Legionary from Londinium and Other Mini-Mysteries
The Roman Mysteries Treasury
From Ostia to Alexandria with Flavia Gemina

THE ROMAN MYSTERY SCROLLS
The Sewer Demon

THE P.K. PINKERTON MYSTERIES
The Case of the Deadly Desperados
The Case of the Good-looking Corpse

The ROMAN MYSTERIES

BOOK V

The Dolphins of Laurentum

CAROLINE LAWRENCE

Orion
Children's Books

First published in Great Britain in 2003
by Orion Children's Books
Paperback edition first published in 2003 by Dolphin Paperbacks
Reissued in 2012 by Orion Children's Books
a division of the Orion Publishing Group Ltd
Orion House
5 Upper St Martin's Lane
London WC2H 9EA

An Hachette UK company

Printed in Great Britain by Clays Ltd, St Ives plc

The Orion Publishing Group's policy is to use papers that are natural,
renewable and recyclable products made from wood grown in sustainable
forests. The logging and manufacturing processes are expected to
conform to the environmental regulations of the country of origin.

www.romanmysteries.com
www.orionbooks.co.uk

To Jan-Theo, Bill, Barbara,
Eric, Silvano, Domenico
and all my other cyber-buddies
from the Ostia website

ITALY IN AD 79
(after the eruption of Vesuvius)

N

Rome

Ostia — River Tiber
— Laurentum

Neapolis
Herculaneum
Misenum — Pompeii
Surrentum — Stabia

Towns destroyed in the
eruption of Vesuvius
are shown in grey

Sicily

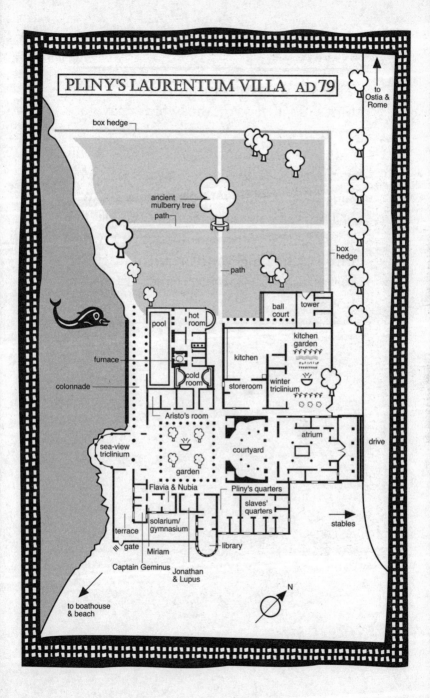

PLINY'S LAURENTUM VILLA AD 79

box hedge

ancient
mulberry tree
path

path

box
hedge

to
Ostia &
Rome

pool

hot
room

ball
court

tower

furnace

colonnade

cold
room

Aristo's room

kitchen

kitchen
garden

storeroom

winter
triclinium

sea-view
triclinium

garden

courtyard

atrium

drive

Flavia & Nubia

Pliny's quarters

slaves'
quarters

terrace

solarium/
gymnasium

library

stables

gate

Miriam

Captain Geminus

Jonathan
& Lupus

N

to boathouse
& beach

This story takes place in Ancient Roman times, so a few of the words may look strange.

If you don't know them, 'Aristo's Scroll' at the back of the book will tell you what they mean and how to pronounce them.

This story contains descriptions of 'free diving', a very dangerous activity which involves holding your breath underwater for as long as possible. Don't try this at home.

SCROLL I

Lupus was drumming.

He sat on the wooden floor of the small bedroom and played his goatskin drum: one beat with his right hand, another with his left. His eyes were closed but in his head he clearly saw the pattern he was making. The hits were small black pebbles, the no-hits were white pebbles. He played the pattern, built up the white and black pebbles and then entwined them in a plait. Just like the black and white mosaic chips in the floor of the triclinium downstairs.

When he wove drum patterns, it drove everything else from his mind. And that was good. The mosaic rhythm lifted him up and carried him along. He was only aware of the ache in his forearms and the tingling in the tips of his fingers and the pattern unwinding in his head.

'Lupus!'

The voice had been calling him for some time now.

He opened his eyes.

Jonathan was sitting on his low bed, tuning a Syrian barbiton.

'Enough warm-up,' said his friend with a grin. 'Let's play.'

Lupus nodded and looked at Jonathan hard. Sometimes, when he'd been drumming, it was as if he'd been dreaming. And when he stopped it was like coming out of a trance: everything looked strange.

His friend Jonathan looked strange.

Maybe it was because Jonathan's hair, once thick and curly, was now shorn to a soft dark stubble. Maybe it was because he'd lost weight, and his dark eyes looked huge in his face. Maybe it was because the brand on his left shoulder was still red and swollen.

Jonathan ben Mordecai had recently turned eleven. He seemed older than his age. Lupus felt older than his own eight and a half years, too. He hadn't felt like a child since his tongue had been cut out.

Lupus watched Jonathan settle the smooth wooden bulb of the instrument between his bare feet and support the long neck with his hands, one over, one under.

He heard the deep note as Jonathan began to thumb the fattest string. The sound was sweet and round. It needed a drumbeat that sounded not like pebbles, but like something softer, rounder, more muted.

Lupus picked up the new drumstick he'd found at Flavia's.

He gave the drum an experimental tap and nodded

in satisfaction at the sound. Perfect. He found the beat and started to weave a new pattern, holding the drumstick in his right hand and using the palm of his left.

'Lupus!' Jonathan was staring at him in horror.

Lupus stopped drumming and gave Jonathan his bug-eyed look: What?

'What on earth are you using as a drumstick?'

Lupus held up the sponge-stick and shrugged, as if to say: It's a sponge-stick.

'Where did you get it?'

Lupus tilted his head towards Flavia's house next door.

'Lupus. Do you know what that is? I mean, what it's used for?'

Lupus shook his head.

Jonathan sighed. 'I know you used to be a half-wild beggar-boy,' he said. 'But you've been living with us for nearly four months now. You're practically a civilised Roman. You're sure you don't know what that sponge-stick is used for?'

Lupus shook his head again. And frowned.

Jonathan leaned forward and grinned. 'It's for wiping your bottom after you've been to the latrine.'

'Flavia!' bellowed a voice from the latrine. 'Where's the sponge-stick?'

Flavia Gemina looked at her ex-slave-girl Nubia.

3

They shrugged at one another, got up and went out of their bedroom onto the balcony.

'I don't know, Uncle Gaius!' Flavia yelled down into the sunny courtyard garden. 'Isn't it there? In the beaker of vinegar?'

'No!' came a grumpy voice from the latrine.

Flavia leaned further over the polished rail and called out, 'Do you want me to grab you some leaves from the fig tree?'

'I'll do it!' said Alma the cook, coming into view. She peered up at the two girls suspiciously.

'You two aren't wearing eyeliner, are you?'

'Um, no!' Flavia hastily pulled Nubia back into their room. Not only were they wearing kohl around their eyes, but they had done up their hair and put on all the jewellery they owned. They were trying on their outfits for Miriam's betrothal supper, although the date had still not been set.

Nubia was wearing a peach shift over a lemon-yellow tunic. 'Flavia . . .' she said slowly, as she brushed her finger against the wine dregs at the bottom of an empty wine-cup, 'what is betrothal supper?'

Flavia was smoothing her own grey silk shift over the sky-blue tunic and admiring the combination. 'Well, it's usually when the parents arrange the marriage of a man and a girl. There's a celebration banquet and the man holds the girl's hand in front of

4

everybody and then he gives her a ring. After that they set the date for the wedding. Alma told me the wedding might be a week later, or a month later or even ten years later, if the couple are very young when they're betrothed. Sometimes the girl is younger than we are.'

Flavia sat beside a small oak table on a folding stool. Nubia sat on a similar stool, facing her former mistress.

'Do you think Miriam and Gaius will wait a year or two later?' Nubia leaned forward and brushed her finger lightly over Flavia's cheekbone.

'I don't think so. First, because of the volcano. Aristo says it reminded everyone that they won't live forever. And second, because they're passionately in love. Alma says it's a bad omen.'

'The volcano?'

'No, that they're in love. She says marrying for love is always a bad idea.' Flavia peered into her highly polished silver mirror. 'No. That's too dark. Brush a bit off.'

Nubia thumbed the wine dregs off Flavia's cheek, leaving just the hint of a blush.

'That's better,' said Flavia, and stroked some of the powdered wine onto Nubia's cheekbone. Then she leaned back on her stool and narrowed her eyes.

'No. Your skin's too dark. It doesn't show up,' said Flavia. She sat forward again. 'Where you grew up, do the parents choose your husband or do you?' she asked.

Nubia covered her smile with her hand. 'We choose, and our parents say yes or no.'

'Now do my mouth,' said Flavia, pushing her lips out.

'Oh, very nice!' came a voice from underneath Flavia's low bed.

'Jonathan!' Flavia squealed and the silver mirror clattered to the floor. 'How long have you been under there?'

Jonathan wriggled out from underneath the bed and grinned up at her. His nutmeg-coloured tunic was grey with fluff and there was brick dust in the stubble of his cropped hair.

'You need to remind Alma to dust under the beds,' he remarked, standing up and brushing off the dust balls.

'Stop!' cried Flavia. 'You'll get our clothes dirty!'

Jonathan ignored Flavia. 'Come on, Lupus,' he said. 'You can come out now.'

'Lupus is under there, too?' Flavia and Nubia exchanged horrified glances. Flavia stood up and folded her arms. Have you two been spying on us? We finished lessons over an hour ago. How long have you been under there?' she repeated.

'Not long.' Jonathan helped Lupus to his feet. Lupus grinned at them. He was wearing his favourite

6

sea-green tunic and had slicked his dark hair back from his forehead with laurel-scented oil. Because Lupus couldn't speak, he always carried a wax tablet with him. Now he opened this tablet with a flourish and thrust it in the girls' faces:

SURPRISE!

With his other hand he held out the sponge-stick.

'Where did you find that?' cried Flavia. 'And how did you –?'

'Shhh!' said Jonathan. 'We don't want anyone else to know about our secret entrance.'

'You mean you came in through the wall?' Flavia's grey eyes widened.

Jonathan nodded. 'My bedroom is right next to yours. Whenever I can't sleep I pick at the plaster. I haven't been sleeping very well since we got back from Rome and I've picked off quite a bit of it. Lupus and I spent all day yesterday getting the mortar out from between the bricks and we've made a way through.'

'Jonathan! How exciting! Let's not tell anybody else,' Flavia breathed. 'Not even your father or Miriam.'

'That's why I've been telling you to be quiet.' Jonathan rolled his eyes.

Flavia sucked a loose strand of her light brown hair

thoughtfully. 'We'll have to think of a secret signal for when we want to come through. How about three taps on the wall?'

Jonathan shook his head. 'Everybody knocks three times,' he said. 'How about four? One for each of us.'

'Excellent idea,' said Flavia.

Lupus gave them a thumbs-up.

At that moment they all heard four distinct raps at the front door of the house. The friends looked at each other, wide-eyed.

'You two stay here. Out of sight!' hissed Flavia. She and Nubia rushed back to the balcony and peered down into the garden.

Flavia's uncle Gaius was standing by the fountain, washing his hands. As he shook the drops from his fingers and turned towards the entrance of the house, Caudex the door-slave staggered into the garden, half-carrying and half-supporting a beggar.

The man wore a tattered tunic and had bandages instead of sandals on his feet. His legs were covered with red sores. His hair was matted and his beard ragged. The beggar was tall, but painfully thin. From her vantage point on the balcony above, Flavia couldn't make out his expression, but it looked as though he was drunk.

'Caudex,' she scolded, starting down the stairs, 'what on earth are you doing? You can't just let any –'

Alma screamed.

8

'Great Jupiter's eyebrows!' exclaimed Gaius, and rushed forward to help Caudex.

Scuto was sniffing the beggar's legs and wagging his tail.

'All lost,' the stranger croaked. 'Ship sunk and everything lost.' As Flavia reached the bottom step, he lifted his head and looked at her. His eyes above the peeling, sunburned cheeks were the same grey-blue as hers, and already tears were filling them.

'Pater!' Flavia gripped the railing with one hand. 'Pater, is it you?'

'Yes, my little owl,' said the sea captain Marcus Flavius Geminus.

Then he collapsed.

SCROLL II

Jonathan's father, Doctor Mordecai ben Ezra, looked up at the people crowding into the bedroom doorway.

'He's still unconscious,' said Mordecai, straightening up from the bedside of Flavia's father. 'From the looks of him, he's suffering from hunger and exposure. It's obvious he's been shipwrecked.'

The doctor rinsed his hands in the copper bowl which his daughter Miriam held.

'I would guess that the cuts on his legs and feet were made by sharp coral.' Mordecai dried his hands on the linen towel over Miriam's arm. 'And I'm afraid they're infected. If we don't act immediately,' he glanced at Flavia's father and lowered his voice, 'we may have to amputate his feet.'

Mordecai spoke Latin with an accent and Nubia didn't understand the word he had just uttered. 'What is amputate?' she asked Flavia.

'Cut off.' Flavia's face was very pale.

'Just tell us what to do.' Gaius stepped forward and looked down at his unconscious twin brother.

'Will you go to the market with Miriam, Gaius? I'll

make her a list of healing foods. She'll know which stalls are most likely to have them. Also, when he wakes up, he'll need lots of liquids. Alma, can you make him chicken soup?'

'Of course, Doctor Mordecai.' Alma looked relieved to have something to do and retreated from the dim bedroom.

'Just broth, to start,' called Mordecai after her. 'Plenty of garlic.'

'Right you are,' came her voice, already halfway downstairs.

'Aristo, can you buy some strips of linen? His wounds will need a fresh dressing.'

'Right away,' said Flavia's tutor, a young Greek with curly hair the colour of bronze. He, too, hurried out of the room.

'Flavia. Nubia.' Mordecai turned to the girls. 'Go down to the beach and fill some buckets with sea-water, as clear as possible.'

The girls nodded.

'When you get back you must sponge his feet and legs with the seawater. It won't be a pleasant job, I'm afraid.'

'That's all right, Doctor Mordecai,' said Flavia and then turned to Nubia. 'Is that all right?'

Nubia nodded.

'Better take Caudex as your bodyguard,' added Mordecai.

'What about us, father?' asked Jonathan. 'What can we do?'

Mordecai looked at the boys, his heavy-lidded eyes as dark as the turban above them. 'You have the most unpleasant job of all,' he said. 'I want you to search the gutters of the meat market. Bring me back some nice young maggots. And make sure they're still alive.'

Nubia stood on Ostia's hot beach for a moment, just where the small waves washed up onto the shore. She liked the feel of the water sucking the sand from under her feet. It tickled. And it was deliciously refreshing to have the blue water cooling her legs. She had changed back into one of her ordinary tunics – the faded apricot one – because it was short enough to allow her to wade in up to her knees.

She used to hate the sea. For most of her life she had lived in the desert. Her first glimpse of the sea had been at the port of Alexandria, when the slave-dealer Venalicius angrily pushed a girl from her clan into its blue depths. The girl had still been chained and she had drowned before Nubia's eyes.

But now that Lupus had taught her to swim, Nubia was no longer afraid of the sea. She moved forward, beyond the little waves that foamed up onto the sand, and lowered the wooden bucket into the water. When it was full, she turned back to the shore.

Her puppy Nipur was sniffing something on the beach. Since the volcano, bits of flotsam and jetsam had been washed ashore almost daily, some of it very unpleasant. Flavia was already there, her bucket filled, also staring down at the object.

'What is it?' said Nubia, splashing back towards the beach.

'Only a medusa,' said Flavia.

'A what?' Nubia looked at the transparent blob with its tangle of greyish-white strings.

'A jellyfish. Don't touch it! It can still sting, even though it's dead. They call them medusas because the tentacles look like Medusa's snaky hair.'

Nubia nodded. Flavia was one of the cleverest people she knew. She was always reading scrolls and knew almost as much about Greek mythology as their tutor Aristo.

Scuto came up to investigate, his tail wagging and his new ball in his mouth. He gave the jellyfish a quick sniff and then retreated. He knew from experience what they could do.

'Filled your bucket?' said Flavia.

Nubia nodded.

'Then let's get back.'

'I can't believe how hot it is for October,' said Jonathan, as he and Lupus slipped behind the stalls of Ostia's meat market.

Lupus grunted. The air above the white stone pavement shimmered with heat and the stench of blood and rotting meat filled his nostrils.

Jonathan's puppy Tigris strained at his rope lead, nose down, urgently following an invisible trail.

'Good boy,' said Jonathan. 'Find the maggots! Ugh! It smells revolting here. Still, I suppose it's good maggot weather.' He ignored an over-the-shoulder glare of a fat pork butcher and scratched the stubble on his head. 'I wonder why my father wants maggots? I don't know of any balms or medicines which have maggots as an ingredient . . .'

Tigris barked, startling a group of feral cats who had been scavenging in the gutter. The cats scattered, then turned to watch the boys from a safe distance. Lupus squatted to examine the object of their attention. Tigris came forward to sniff it and Lupus gently pushed the puppy away.

'Ugh!' Jonathan lifted Tigris into his arms. 'Why did God make flies? And maggots . . .' He gazed down at the rotting chicken leg. Dozens of white maggots writhed in the rancid meat.

Lupus pulled out his handkerchief, a rather grubby one that smelled faintly of lemon blossom, and carefully wrapped the chicken leg in it. Then he stood and nodded.

'Well done, Tigris,' said Jonathan, and kissed his puppy's nose. 'You're a good maggot-hunter.'

Lupus patted Tigris, too, and the boys started back towards Green Fountain Street.

As Lupus and Jonathan made their way through the crowded forum, Lupus glanced warily around. In his begging days he had learned to be constantly alert, always aware of his surroundings and any possible danger. Old habits died hard.

It was almost noon and the forum was crowded with people finishing their day's work before returning home for a light meal and short siesta. It was still as hot and heavy as summer and a layer of charcoal smoke from the morning sacrifices hung over the forum. Everyone blamed the eruption of Vesuvius two months earlier for the unusually hot autumn and lack of rain.

On Lupus's left rose the gleaming white temple of the Capitoline triad: Jupiter, Juno and Minerva. On his right stood the basilica where only a few weeks earlier Jonathan's father Mordecai had been imprisoned for hiding a suspected assassin. According to Miriam, they had officially released Mordecai by having a scribe announce that he had been cleared of blame and was free to go.

A similar ceremony was taking place now on the steps of the basilica. Lupus glanced over to see who was being released.

The prisoner was a barrel-chested man in a filthy

grey tunic. His head was wrapped in linen strips, stained with dried blood. He was facing the scribe and the magistrate with his back to Lupus, but as he turned Lupus's stomach writhed as if it were as full of maggots as his handkerchief.

The man gazing around the forum with a blind eye and a twisted smile was the person Lupus hated most in the world: Venalicius the slave-dealer.

SCROLL III

'Venalicius is here in Ostia!' cried Jonathan, and rushed past Caudex to cry out again, 'Flavia! Where are you?'

'Upstairs in pater's room,' came Flavia's voice.

Jonathan took the wooden stairs two at a time, with Lupus and the dogs close behind him.

'Flavia!' Jonathan cried, then stopped as he saw she had her finger to her lips.

Marcus Flavius Geminus was sitting up in bed and Jonathan's father was standing beside him with a razor-sharp blade.

'Hello, Jonathan. Hello, Lupus.' Marcus's voice was little more than a whisper.

'Hello, Captain Geminus,' said Jonathan. 'Welcome home.'

Lupus nodded his greeting.

Jonathan glanced down at Flavia and Nubia, who were sponging Marcus's wounded feet. Then he wished he hadn't.

'Not a pretty sight, is it?' whispered Captain Geminus.

Jonathan swallowed and tried to smile.

'Did you get the . . . what I asked for?' said Mordecai.

Lupus nodded and held out his handkerchief.

Jonathan stared at the razor in his father's hand.

'You're not going to amputate his feet, are you?'

Mordecai smiled. 'No, I was just about to shave him. But now I have something more important to do.' He put down the razor and turned to Captain Geminus. 'I must ask you to put aside your prejudices, Marcus. I have used this method before and it is remarkable. I would like to put maggots in the infected wounds on your feet.'

'Ugh!' squealed Flavia. 'No!'

'Flavia,' croaked her father. 'Let the doctor finish.'

Mordecai took a deep breath. 'The maggots eat the dead flesh . . . the rotting flesh. But they do not eat the healthy skin. In a few days the maggots will be fat and the remaining flesh will be whole and healthy and ready to heal.' Mordecai opened Lupus's handkerchief and nodded with satisfaction. 'I will only do this,' he continued, 'if you consent. However, I must warn you, I believe it is either maggots or amputation.'

They all looked at one another and the four friends breathed a collective sigh of relief as Captain Geminus whispered, 'Maggots, please.'

'What were you in such a hurry to tell us?' Flavia

asked Jonathan a short time later. Mordecai had applied the maggots to her father's wounds and bound his torn feet loosely with strips of clean linen. Shaved and shorn, her father had drunk a bowlful of chicken soup and was now fast asleep in his darkened bedroom.

Downstairs in Flavia's cool, marble-floored triclinium Doctor Mordecai, Aristo and the four friends were sipping mint tea.

'We wanted to tell you that Venalicius is here,' Jonathan said. 'Lupus and I just saw him being set free on the steps of the basilica.'

'Venalicius!' Flavia and Nubia stared at one another in horror. 'But he was arrested in Surrentum after he tried to buy freeborn children as slaves. Why is he back in Ostia?'

Mordecai put down his cup of mint tea. 'They brought him back here to stand trial,' he said. 'Ostia is his home and his base of operations.'

'You knew about this?' said Flavia.

Mordecai nodded.

'You knew Venalicius was in Ostia?' Jonathan stared at his father.

'Yes. I knew.'

Lupus gave an odd choking sound, and Aristo patted him on the back.

Because Lupus was tongueless, sometimes food and drink went down the wrong way. Apparently not this time, thought Flavia, for Lupus writhed away from Aristo's patting and pointed at Mordecai accusingly.

'Yes, Lupus,' said Mordecai quietly. 'As I think you've just guessed, my cellmate last month was Venalicius.'

'What?' cried Flavia.

'Last month,' repeated Mordecai. 'While you were in Rome. You remember that I spent a week in the basilica after I was arrested? Well, I wasn't alone.'

Aristo said something to Mordecai in Greek and the doctor replied in the same language.

Lupus stared at them in disbelief, then snarled and lifted his empty cup as if to smash it against a wall. Jonathan caught the younger boy's wrist and said:

'Whoa, Lupus! What's the matter?'

Lupus gave Mordecai a withering look, slammed his cup onto the table and stomped out into the garden.

'Why were you speaking Greek and what did you say?' asked Flavia. She stared out into the bright garden at Lupus, who was pacing angrily back and forth under the dappled shade of the fig tree.

'Last month,' said Aristo, 'Lupus and I brought Mordecai some medical supplies, when he was being held in the basilica. I just asked Mordecai if he had used them to bandage Venalicius' ear, the one Lupus nearly cut off.'

'And I said that I had,' added Mordecai. 'That

sometimes an act of kindness speaks more than a thousand words, and that no man is beyond redemption until he dies.'

'I'm sorry, Flavia,' said Aristo. 'I know you hate it when I speak Greek. But Lupus hates Venalicius so much that he tried to kill him last month. I was trying not to upset him.'

'It didn't work,' remarked Jonathan.

'Do you know,' said Flavia slowly, 'I think Lupus understood every word you said!'

Lupus needed to get out of the house. He needed to breathe. He needed to think.

He knew Scuto's lead hung just inside the kitchen doorway. Alma smiled at him from the hearth as he pulled it off its nail. It was rare that Scuto actually went on the lead, but its jingle always alerted him that it was walk-time.

Immediately four wagging dogs appeared at Lupus's feet: big black Ferox, the two smaller black puppies and medium-sized Scuto, ball in mouth.

'Are you going to take the dogs out, Lupus?' called Flavia from the triclinium.

Lupus nodded and glanced over at them. They were all watching him, probably talking about him, too.

'Thanks, Lupus,' called Jonathan.

Lupus ignored them and unbolted the back door.

Flavia's house was built against Ostia's town wall, and the back door was built into this thick wall. It led straight into the graveyard and for security reasons there was no latch on the outside.

Jonathan – whose house was virtually a mirror image of Flavia's – had invented a small wooden wedge to prop his door open. He had made a similar one for Flavia's house. Lupus now kicked this wedge into place and let the door almost close behind him. Then he stepped outside the town into the hot afternoon.

Scuto and the two puppies had already raced through the door and now sped through the golden grasses towards their favourite umbrella pine. Ferox, still recovering from a knife wound to the chest, limped beside Lupus as he made his way past the tombs of the dead towards the Laurentum Road.

Once, not so long ago, Lupus had tormented Ferox by slinging stones at his rump. But Ferox's wound had made him gentle. He had either forgotten or forgiven the offence. Lupus ruffled the top of Ferox's head and the big dog rolled his eyes back and panted. His tail went steadily back and forth.

Strange, thought Lupus, how a wound can make a gentle creature fierce and a fierce creature gentle.

Presently they reached the road and Ferox squatted in some horse grass to do his business.

Lupus discreetly turned away. He closed his eyes

for a moment and inhaled the spicy scent of the sun-bleached grasses and pine resin. The buzzing of the cicadas was thin and brisk. Autumn was coming. His heart had stopped pounding and he no longer felt quite as sick as he had when Mordecai had confessed showing kindness towards Venalicius.

A moist nose butted his knee in mute appeal. It was Scuto. Flavia had brought her dog a ball as a souvenir from Rome and he was besotted with it. Scuto dropped this ball in the dusty pine needles at Lupus's feet, then backed away and gazed up at Lupus expectantly.

Lupus picked up the ball and threw it hard towards the dunes. Scuto and the two puppies pursued it joyfully and Ferox ambled across the road after them.

As Lupus followed, he allowed himself to remember his first ball. It had also been leather, sewn from two pieces of pigskin and filled with dried lentils. His parents had given it to him on his sixth birthday, a beautiful mild day in the middle of February, two and a half years ago.

Lupus and his father had stood before the bright sea, laughing and tossing the ball back and forth. With each catch they had taken a step away from one another. Eventually his father had become a dark silhouette against the dazzling water behind him. Then Lupus's mother had called them and presently half the village had gathered beneath their grape arbour to feast on suckling pig. Lupus still remembered the salty sweetness of the meat, roasted on a spit and glazed with honey, a rare delicacy on the island. That was when he still had a tongue and could taste food.

He remembered how happy his father had been that day: half closing his green eyes and showing his white teeth whenever he laughed. And his mother Melissa. So beautiful and full of love.

A few months later all that had been taken from him by the man who called himself Venalicius. Lupus's heart started pounding again. He bent to pick up Scuto's ball, then threw it with a grunt of rage, as hard as he could. He and Ferox followed the dogs and presently they topped a dune with a view of the water.

Lupus clenched his fists and stared out at the Tyrrhenian Sea, its blue so deep it was almost black. Many times before he had promised the gods he would get revenge. This time he silently vowed to do something about it.

SCROLL IV

The next day, Lupus paid a visit to the Baths of Thetis. He knew most of the people who visited this baths complex. In his begging days, before he had consented to live with Jonathan, the bath attendants had let him sleep by the furnace and scavenge scraps of food left behind by the clientele.

Sometimes a young changing-room slave had given Lupus a few coppers to help him guard the clothes. Now this same slave – his name was Umidus – stared down at Lupus with a frown.

'Lupus? Is it you?' Umidus's voice was muffled; he had a cleft palate and could only speak with difficulty.

Lupus nodded and took out his wax tablet:

NEED SOME HELP?

Umidus scratched his big head. 'I hardly recognised you. You look like a young gentleman! And you can read and write? I wish I could!'

Lupus dropped the tablet and gestured round at the

changing-room, then rubbed his forefinger and thumb together.

'You want to earn a few coins? All right. You can keep any tips you get.'

Lupus nodded with satisfaction. He didn't want Umidus to suspect his real reason for coming – to hire an assassin.

It was here in the Baths of Thetis that Lupus had first seen the man named Gamala.

The Gamala family had lived in Ostia for many generations, and were well-respected. But the man who called himself Gnaeus Lucilius Gamala was not a native of Ostia. He was a foreign relation of the Gamala family. He spoke Latin with an accent. Some said he came from Judaea, others said Syria. But everyone knew he had done something criminal before settling down in Ostia; the scars of the whip on his back were there for all to see. Recently Lupus had developed a theory. He reckoned Gamala had been a *sicarius*: a member of the elite Jewish assassination squad.

Lupus was about to test this hunch. He remembered that Gamala usually came in with the first wave of male customers.

As the gong began to clang noon, the double doors of the baths opened and the first group of men entered the pale blue changing-room. Lupus's heart beat faster as he saw the person he was waiting for.

Gamala was tall and lithe, with thick black hair, a nose like an eagle's beak and keen brown eyes. He was alone, accompanied by neither friend nor slave, and he moved over to his usual niche with a fluid grace. Once there, he stripped off, folded his tunic, and placed it in the cube-shaped recess in the blue wall. His belt and money pouch went on top. Before he turned to go, he tossed Lupus a small copper coin.

As Gamala strode towards the palaestra for a pre-bath workout, Lupus studied the pale scars on his retreating back. He counted twenty separate strokes before Gamala disappeared through the arched door-way.

Lupus knew the whip-marks were not proof that Gamala was an assassin. Punishment for that crime was crucifixion. But they indicated that he might have been a Zealot, a Jew who had rebelled against Roman rule in Judaea. Lupus also remembered what Jonathan had told him recently: even a retired *sicarius* never feels safe without his weapon.

When the changing-room was empty, Lupus stepped up onto the plaster-covered bench which ran round the room. He leaned into Gamala's niche and began to examine the contents. Behind him, across the black and white mosaic floor, Umidus the bath-slave uttered a cry of protest. Lupus looked over his shoulder and gave a small shake of his head to say: Don't worry; I'm just looking.

Quickly, Lupus patted Gamala's tunic, sandals and coin purse. It was only when he examined the last item that he found what he was looking for. Cleverly concealed in a secret pocket of Gamala's leather belt was a small knife. It was razor-sharp and curved like a sickle.

Flavia sat in a chair beside her father's bed and gazed down at his face. He had slept through the whole night and most of the morning, then woken at noon to take some more chicken broth. Now he was sleeping again.

The room was dim and relatively cool. Quiet, too, now that most of Ostia was taking a siesta. The only sounds she could hear were the faint strains of Jonathan practising his barbiton next door and the thin buzz of the cicadas from the umbrella pines.

Every morning over the previous two weeks Flavia had stood before the household shrine and vowed that if the gods brought her father back she would be a good, dutiful Roman daughter.

But it seemed the gods had returned a different father from the one who had sailed away. This father looked frail and helpless. His eyelashes lay pale against his sunburnt skin and his cracked lips were slightly parted in sleep. He looked like a boy.

Or maybe she was the one who was different.

So much had happened in the two months since he had sailed out of Pompeii's harbour. She had been to Stabia, Surrentum and Rome. She had survived a volcano, pirates and assassins. She had witnessed death and birth, grief and joy. People her father had never even met – Vulcan, Clio, Pulchra, Sisyphus, even the Emperor himself – had become her friends.

And she had met *him*.

Flavia looked down at the object she held carefully in her lap.

A dutiful Roman daughter should marry and have children. Soon her father would be thinking about arranging a suitable match for her. How could she tell him she would never marry? That she would never give him grandchildren? That her heart belonged to someone she could never have?

Flavia sighed, and lifted her eyes. The thread of afternoon light around the curtained doorway blurred, then cleared as she let a few hot tears spill onto her cheek. She felt very old and very wise.

With another deep sigh she turned her gaze back to the cup and to the image of the handsome god painted inside.

Jonathan stopped playing his barbiton and frowned. He thought he heard his sister shouting. But he wasn't sure. He didn't think he had ever heard her raise her voice before. He heard a man's voice, too, but he knew his father had gone out to see a patient.

'We'll never get married!' came his sister's voice distinctly from the garden.

Slowly Jonathan lifted the barbiton from his lap and set it beside him on the bed. Three steps took him to the bedroom doorway.

'Of course we will.' Jonathan recognised the voice of Flavia's uncle Gaius. 'Just as soon as I find somewhere for us to live.'

Jonathan moved quietly to the rail of the balcony above their inner garden.

Below him, Miriam and Gaius stood face to face in the shade of the fig tree.

'With what money?' Miriam cried. 'You have hardly any left. Why won't you use my dowry? I have twenty gold coins.'

'I don't want to use your dowry,' said Gaius. 'That's your security.'

'But I don't want security. I want to be married to you and I want us to live in our own house. A house with a garden.'

'I refuse to live on your money.' Gaius ran his hand through his light brown hair. 'I have my pride.'

'Oh!' cried Miriam in disgust. 'You and your masculine pride.' She turned away from him and hung her head so that her dark curls hid her face.

Gaius sighed and touched her shoulder. 'Miriam,'

he said. 'I love you more than anything in the world. I've waited my whole life to find someone like you, waited till I'm an old man.'

'You're not an old man.' Miriam turned back to him and tried not to smile. 'You're only thirty-one.'

'I'm an old man,' repeated Gaius with a grin, pulling her into his arms. 'And I should be able to take care of you, to provide for you . . .'

Miriam lifted her face and for a moment Jonathan saw how beautiful his mother must have been at fourteen.

Gaius's grin faded. 'I love you so much,' he whispered. And lowered his head to kiss her.

Jonathan watched with a mixture of horror and fascination. Should he step back into his room? But what if they noticed the movement and accused him of spying on them?

He needn't have worried. They were oblivious to everything except each other.

Lupus's head jerked up. He must have dozed off. He was sitting in the pale blue changing-room of the Baths of Thetis, waiting to hire an assassin.

Had he missed Gamala? No. A quick glance showed the man's clothes still in his niche.

Lupus stood and stretched and looked round for Umidus. The young bath-slave was sitting across the room on the plaster bench that ran right round the wall. His head was tipped back and his open eyes stared unseeing at the circular skylight of the domed ceiling.

Lupus took a step forward and found his knees were trembling.

Umidus the bath-slave appeared to be quite dead.

SCROLL V

As Lupus stared down at the dead bath-attendant he heard someone chuckling behind him.

He whirled to find himself face to face with a probable assassin.

'You think he's dead, don't you?' said Gamala, towelling his hair. 'Have a closer look.' He turned and walked over to his cubicle.

Lupus looked down at Umidus. Was the slave still breathing? He glanced back at Gamala, who was slipping on his tunic.

'Gave me quite a fright once, too,' said Gamala with a grin. 'But he's just sleeping. I knew another man like that once. In Judaea. Slept with his eyes wide open. His wife couldn't take it. She divorced him in the end.'

Lupus looked back down at the bath attendant. Although the young slave's eyes were wide open, Lupus could now see his chest rising and falling gently. He breathed a sigh of relief.

'He probably just had a late night. Let him sleep.' Gamala sat on the bench and began lacing up his sandals. The changing-room was still deserted.

Lupus suddenly realised that if he were going to act, it must be now.

His heart thumping, Lupus approached Gamala. With his left hand he gripped the leather pouch which held all his worldly wealth: two gold coins, each worth a hundred sestercii. In his right hand he held his wax tablet. On it he had drawn a sickle-shaped knife and underneath he had printed in his neatest writing:

HOW MUCH TO KILL VENALICIUS THE SLAVE-DEALER?

*

'We had to leave Pliny's body on the beach,' said Flavia from her seat at the table.

It was dinner time. She and her friends were telling her father about the eruption of Vesuvius six weeks earlier.

'The sulphur fumes would have killed us if we hadn't left right away,' added Jonathan. 'I nearly died.'

'And Frustilla did die,' said Gaius, who was reclining next to Miriam.

'Poor old Frustilla.' Captain Geminus put down his bowl of chicken soup. After nearly a day and a half of sleeping he had asked to dine with the others. Caudex had carried him downstairs and propped him up on cushions. 'And poor Admiral Pliny. What a way to die.'

'But he died a hero,' said Flavia, taking a bite of salad and sucking the honey and vinegar dressing from her fingers.

Beside her Lupus nodded his agreement, and Jonathan explained: 'Pliny went to Herculaneum to try to save Rectina and then when he couldn't reach the shore he headed south to Stabia. That's where we were.'

'Yes.' Captain Geminus nodded sadly. 'Pliny could have gone back to the safety of the harbour at Misenum. There's no doubt that he was a brave man. I'm sorry I never got to know him better.'

Scuto and the puppies had been sitting attentively below the dining couches hoping for scraps. Suddenly they barked and scampered out of the triclinium.

A few moments later the golden light of late afternoon dimmed as Caudex stepped into the door-way.

'Man here to see you,' he mumbled to nobody in particular. 'Says his name's Pliny.'

'I'm terribly sorry to interrupt your dinner,' said the man who called himself Pliny.

This was not the Pliny she knew, thought Nubia, but a much younger man. She noted the soft fuzz on his upper lip, and guessed he was probably about the age of her eldest brother Taharqo, who was seventeen.

But the youth did bear a strong resemblance to the old admiral: he was short, with the same keen black eyes and pale, rumpled eyebrows. And the set of his small mouth was the same. However, unlike Admiral Pliny, this young man was slim. And he had hair: a thick brown mop of it, which he combed over his forehead.

'You haven't interrupted us.' Gaius slid off the couch and extended his hand. 'We've just started.'

'Please join us,' said Captain Geminus, trying to sit forward, then sinking back onto his cushions.

'That's very kind of you,' said the young man, looking round at them all. 'Allow me to introduce myself. I am Gaius Plinius Caecilius Secundus. I believe you knew my uncle and were with him when he died.'

'You're Pliny's nephew!' cried Flavia.

The young man inclined his head. 'I am indeed the admiral's nephew.'

Nubia nodded to herself. That made sense.

'What a coincidence!' Captain Geminus tried to sit up again and this time he succeeded. 'We were just talking about your uncle, saying how brave he was.'

'Yes,' said the young man and Nubia saw his black eyes grow moist. 'That's why I've come. To hear of his last hours. My uncle's scribe Phrixus said you were all with him at the end.'

'Please,' said Gaius. 'Wash your hands and join us.

Caudex, would you bring the copper basin? And a fresh napkin?'

But Miriam was already on her feet. She smiled at young Pliny and he stared at her open-mouthed. Flushing slightly, Miriam hurried out of the triclinium.

'I'm Gaius Flavius Geminus,' said Flavia's uncle. 'I own – or rather *used* to own – a farm in Stabia. That's my brother Marcus, whose hospitality you're enjoying.'

Captain Geminus gave young Pliny a weak smile from the dining-couch.

'This is Mordecai ben Ezra,' continued Gaius. 'He is the doctor who treated many of your uncle's sailors for burns and cuts. And this,' said Gaius, as Miriam came back into the dining-room, 'this is his daughter Miriam.'

Nubia saw the young man's neck flush as he dipped his hands in the basin Miriam held.

Although Miriam was only fourteen, her beauty was fully developed. Nubia thought she looked particularly lovely this afternoon: she wore a faded lavender tunic with a matching headscarf that allowed her black curls to spill up and over. On her wrist gleamed a silver and amethyst bracelet.

Gaius finished the introductions and invited Pliny's nephew to join him on the central couch beside Miriam.

'Alas! That might not be good idea,' Nubia whispered to Flavia. They watched the young man clamber somewhat awkwardly onto the couch and saw him grow pink as Miriam lowered her slender form next to his.

'Thank you.' Young Pliny accepted a bowl of salad from Alma.

'What would you like to know about your uncle's last hours?' asked Gaius. 'Anything in particular?'

Pliny fished a radish out of his bowl. 'My uncle's scribe Phrixus was with him the whole time. He told me most of what happened. I just wondered if you could add any details. I am writing up an account of his last hours.' He turned to Lupus. 'Are you the boy who brought Rectina's message to my uncle?'

When Lupus nodded, Pliny said, 'You and the blacksmith did an extraordinary thing.'

'But if Lupus hadn't brought the message your uncle might still be alive,' said Jonathan through a mouthful of cucumber, and then stopped crunching as he realised what he'd said.

'No, no,' said Pliny's nephew. 'My uncle had already decided to investigate the phenomenon. This boy's arrival persuaded him to go in a warship, which was a much more sensible means of conveyance.'

Nubia whispered to Flavia, 'I am not understanding him.'

'He said if Lupus hadn't come along, Admiral Pliny would have taken a small boat instead of a big one.'

'Oh,' said Nubia.

'Why didn't you go with your uncle?' Flavia asked

the young man. 'Didn't you want to help him investigate?'

'My uncle had asked me to compose an imaginary letter from Cicero to Livy,' said Pliny. 'I was busy working on that.'

Jonathan raised his eyebrows. 'A mountain ten miles away had just exploded and you stayed in to do your homework?'

Pliny flushed and looked down into his salad bowl, then back up at Jonathan. 'I intend to climb the ladder of honour all the way to the top. Law is the first rung of the ladder. To become a successful lawyer, I must show self-discipline. My assignment seemed important at the time. Besides, when my uncle set out, it wasn't even clear which mountain the smoke was coming from.' He looked around at them all. 'As it happened, I was able to help my mother and the terrified peasants around us. But I very much regret that I couldn't have been with my uncle in his last hours.'

'I don't think there's anything you could have done for him,' said Mordecai gently. 'Your uncle was obviously asthmatic and the fumes were so dense . . . But he was courageous to the end.'

'Phrixus tells me that my uncle actually slept for several hours.'

'Yes!' Jonathan nodded vigorously. 'I had to pass his room on the way to the latrine and I could hear him snoring. Even over the noise of the volcano!'

'What courage!' cried Pliny.

Lupus appeared to have a choking fit but Flavia and Jonathan patted his back until it subsided. Luckily young Pliny didn't notice their amused reaction. His gaze had strayed to Miriam again.

Over the course of the meal, Nubia observed that the young man kept looking at Jonathan's sister. Once he even closed his eyes and inhaled. Somehow she knew it was not the pine-nut and honey omelette he was sniffing.

Near the end of dinner, when the air was cooler and the scents of the garden filled the dining-room, Alma brought in the dessert course of peppered figs and cheese. She was just going out again when the dogs ran barking to the front of the house a second time. Once more, Caudex stood in the wide doorway of the dining-room.

'Another man to see you, master,' he growled. 'Don't like the look of this one.'

Flavia saw her father and uncle exchange glances and then Gaius said, 'I'll go.'

A moment later Gaius was back, looking grim. A short man with greasy black hair and a jutting chin stood beside him, unrolling a papyrus scroll.

'This is an official notice for Marcus Flavius Geminus, sea captain,' he read in a loud, nasal voice. 'From the bankers Rufus and Dexter. Unless you pay the amount of one hundred thousand sestercii by this time tomorrow your house and all its possessions will be seized and sold to pay off this debt.'

'What?' said Marcus, struggling to rise from the couch. 'That's insane! I can't possibly pay that amount. My ship was lost. The cargo, too.'

'Was you insured, sir?' said Greasy-hair.

'No, that is . . . I can raise the money . . . but you must give me time. There was no time limit on that loan.'

'Afraid that's not entirely true, sir. According to this, the amount is payable at the lender's discretion. And that's now.'

'But . . . you can't do that!'

For the first time in her life, Flavia saw panic in her father's eyes.

'Marcus, let me handle this.' Gaius turned to Greasy-hair. 'Where do your employers operate from?'

'I'm only the messenger,' sneered the man, 'I have lots of employers.'

'I mean the bankers Rufus and Dexter. Where can I find them?'

'Banker's stall on the west side of the forum, opposite the little circular temple. But this states quite clearly,' said Greasy-hair with a smirk, 'that unless you pay one hundred thousand sestercii, they're possessing your house tomorrow.'

SCROLL VI

'Great Neptune's beard!' said Marcus, after the messenger left. 'I'm ruined.'

Mordecai rose from his couch, looking grave. 'Gaius, this is the worst thing for your brother. His mental state must remain positive. Is there anything you can do to stop this happening?'

Gaius pushed his hand through his fair hair. 'A month ago I could have paid his debts. But since Vesuvius erupted . . .'

'What about Cordius?' suggested Flavia. 'Your patron?'

'Yes!' said Marcus, then his face fell. 'No. He's away at his estates in Sicily. He always goes to oversee the grape harvest and remains there until the Saturnalia.'

'Or Senator Cornix?' suggested Aristo. 'By the looks of his town-house in Rome, he has money to spare . . .'

Captain Geminus shook his head. 'There's bad blood between us . . .' he murmured.

Flavia took a deep breath. 'Publius Pollius Felix might help us,' she said. 'He's rich. And powerful.'

'He might,' said Gaius, 'but he's in Surrentum. Even if I sent a messenger at dawn it would be a week before I heard anything back.'

'We have to do something!' Flavia blurted out. 'I don't want to leave our house. I love it!' She bit her lip, aware that she wasn't helping.

Sensing her distress, Scuto placed a paw on her leg. Flavia slipped off her chair and put her arms around Scuto's woolly neck. From the couch behind her young Pliny spoke.

'If the worst happens, you can always stay with me. I owe you a debt for your kindness towards my uncle in his last hours. I've inherited his Laurentum villa. It's only a few miles down the coast and I've room enough for all of you.' Here he glanced at Miriam. 'I'd be most honoured if you would be my guests. All of you,' he repeated.

'That's very kind of you,' said Gaius, 'but –'

'– it might be an excellent idea,' Mordecai said to Pliny's nephew. He turned to Gaius. 'May I have a word with you in private?'

'Of course, doctor.' The two of them rose and went out towards the study.

There was an awkward silence in the dining-room as everyone looked at one another. When they realised they could hear Mordecai's accented voice in the study, repeating the phrase 'must remain positive', Jonathan began to hum a little tune, then asked Pliny's nephew if he would like more peppered figs.

A few minutes later Gaius and Mordecai returned.

'Secundus,' said Gaius to the young man.

'Please call me Pliny.'

'Pliny,' said Gaius, 'your offer has come at a good time. My brother needs to recover his strength. And it would be best for the children not to be exposed to this unsettling business. We accept your kind offer. Mordecai and I will stay in Ostia and try to sort out this matter. But can you take Captain Geminus and his household and put them up at your Laurentum villa?'

'My great pleasure,' said the young man. 'Er . . . does that include the doctor's daughter?'

'An excellent idea,' said Mordecai. 'Miriam is almost as skilled as I am. She can look after Marcus. Monitor his progress.'

'And me?' Aristo narrowed his eyes at Pliny. 'Shouldn't I go too?' He looked at Captain Geminus. 'Don't you want me to continue the children's lessons?'

'Lessons?' said Pliny. 'To keep the children occupied? What a good idea.'

'It's an excellent idea,' said Flavia's father from his couch. 'We mustn't interrupt their education just because disaster has struck.'

'Jonathan and Lupus will come, too, won't they?'

Flavia unwrapped her arms from Scuto's neck and stood up.

Mordecai glanced at Gaius, who nodded. 'Of course,' said Mordecai. 'I think it would be better if you all went. Things here could get . . . difficult. Caudex and Alma can stay at my house with Gaius. There will be room if the boys go with Marcus and the girls.'

Gaius turned to Pliny. 'I can't thank you enough for your kind offer,' he said. 'Surely the gods sent you today.'

Pliny glanced at Miriam again and Flavia heard him murmur: 'I am almost tempted to agree.'

Lupus woke instantly. Something was wrong.

It was just before dawn. Through the latticework screen of the bedroom window, the sky showed as grey diamonds in the solid blackness of the wall. It was not the steady sound of Jonathan's breathing that had woken Lupus, but something else.

It came again: four urgent taps on the wall. Their secret signal!

Lupus grunted and threw off the linen sheet that half covered him. He quickly slipped on the tunic he had been wearing the day before and shook Jonathan by the shoulder.

'Mmmf. Whuzzit, Rizpah?' mumbled Jonathan. Tigris's head appeared from beneath Jonathan's sheet as the tapping came again. Lupus dragged the bed away from the wall – with Jonathan and Tigris still in it – and started to pull out the bricks.

'Ow!' Jonathan winced as he lifted himself up on his branded left arm. 'What are you doing, Lupus?'

But Lupus already had one of the bricks out, and now hands were pushing from the other side, widening the hole.

'Jonathan! Lupus!' came Flavia's voice from the other side. 'They're here!'

'Who?' said Jonathan, groggily slipping on his own tunic, back to front. 'Who are here?'

'Bailiffs. Two men, one with a scribe's pen. They're making a list of all the things in the house so that we don't take them.'

'They can't do that, can they?' Jonathan yawned again and helped pull out bricks. The diamonds in the window were already a lighter grey and as Lupus got down on his belly, he could see Flavia's face: a dark smudge with darker smudges where her eyes were. Tigris padded over to investigate and touched noses with his brother Nipur, sniffing from the other side.

'I think they can take almost everything,' hissed Flavia. 'My things, too! And Nubia's! Can we hand them through to you?'

'Of course,' said Jonathan. 'Tigris! Get back!'

'This is the most important one,' whispered Flavia. 'Quickly, before they come upstairs.'

As Jonathan lifted Tigris out of the way, Lupus took the object Flavia had thrust through the wall. It was a smooth, flat ceramic cup with small handles. Suddenly he knew what it was: the elegant Greek kylix which the rich patron Felix had given to Flavia the month before. Lupus put it carefully on the bed and reached for the next object.

More things were coming through: Nubia's flute, her tigers-eye earrings in their original pouch, a silver mirror, two scrolls and Flavia's tambourine.

'Flavia!' said Jonathan suddenly. 'What about all that gold in your store room? The gold you were keeping safe for your father's patron?'

'It's all right,' said Flavia. 'After we caught the thief, Cordius took it back.'

She pushed a large wad of material through the gap. As Lupus put it on the bed he saw it was several silk tunics rolled together.

'They're coming!' hissed Flavia. 'I have to put my bed back. Can you close the gap?'

'Yes!' whispered Jonathan. He was still holding Tigris.

Lupus quickly replaced the bricks. He was just about to fit the last brick into its space when he heard voices and saw the flickering yellow light of an oil-lamp illuminate the floor beneath Flavia's bed. He glanced over his shoulder at Jonathan and then put his eye to the diamond-shaped space where the last brick would go.

Lupus could see the calves of Flavia's legs, silhouetted against the torchlight. Clever girl. She was sitting on the bed.

'We'll make note of all the items in here, too,' said a man's voice.

'Ready,' came the reply, presumably from the scribe.

'Two beds; two folding stools, wood with bronze lion-feet; one oak table. On the table: two wooden combs; two bath-sets; three clay oil-lamps; three scent bottles, one ceramic, one glass and one rock crystal.'

Lupus heard the scraping of items on a table.

'Three necklaces . . . just glass beads,' continued the bailiff, 'one make-up box, six brass hairpins, four ivory hairpins, seven bone hairpins . . . That's everything on the table.'

There was a pause and the torchlight flickered.

'Got a chest here . . . looks like it's made of cedarwood, full of clothes. Two woollen mantles –'

'You can't take our clothes!' Lupus heard Flavia cry.

'I'm afraid we can,' said the scribe's voice. 'They're valuable property.'

The bailiff continued: 'We also have one bronze standing oil-lamp, one woven rug, one slave-girl –'

'No!' cried Flavia fiercely. 'Nubia is not a slave. I set her free last month and my witness is Publius Pollius Felix. Don't you dare put her on that list!'

There was a pause and then the bailiff continued.

'Two watchdogs: one medium-sized mongrel with pale brown fur and one black mastiff puppy.'

'Mongrel!' Flavia's voice sputtered with fury. 'He's not a . . . anyway, the dogs belong to our next-door-neighbour, not to me.'

'Both of them?' Lupus could hear the sneer in the bailiff's voice. 'I find that hard to believe.'

'Yes,' Flavia lied. 'Both of them.'

'We can verify that later. Now, if you girls don't mind moving, we'll just have a quick look under the beds.'

SCROLL VII

'Jonathan, it was terrible!' Flavia's face was red and blotched. 'They just came right in as if they owned everything already. And they tried to take Nubia. And Scuto and Nipur!'

'I know. We heard everything.' Jonathan patted Flavia on the back. Dawn was just breaking and they were in Jonathan's house, sitting on the striped silk divan in his father's study.

Lupus scribbled something on his wax tablet and held it up:

AT LEAST WE GOT BRICK BACK IN

Flavia blew her nose and nodded.

Nubia added, 'It is good you make that hole in the wall yesterday.'

Jonathan gave her a rueful smile. 'Yes, it was.'

Flavia blew her nose again. 'Is my kylix safe?'

'Yes, we've got your precious cup,' said Jonathan.

'And I've got the mint tea.' Miriam came in with a tray of steaming beakers.

'Thank you, Miriam.' Flavia smiled through her tears. 'Mint tea always makes me feel better.' She warmed her hands on the side of the beaker and then took a sip. 'Mmmm. Nice and sweet.'

'Better?' asked Jonathan.

'A little,' said Flavia, and took another sip of the fragrant brew. 'Where's your father?'

'He went next door, just after you arrived. I think he's helping Gaius supervise the rest of the inventory.' He slurped his own tea.

'Oh, Jonathan!' Flavia's lip began to tremble. 'What are we going to do? Our beautiful house with its secret garden. And Scuto's jasmine bush. And the fig tree.'

'And fountain,' added Nubia.

'And pater's study and all my scrolls . . .'

Jonathan could tell she was about to cry again. He had to do something.

Suddenly he jumped up from the divan. 'Wait! A brilliant plan!'

'Yes?'

'That's what we need,' said Jonathan, sitting down again. 'A brilliant plan.'

There was a moment of silence. Then everyone laughed.

'Oh, Jonathan!' Flavia said. 'What would we do without you?'

He shrugged and grinned at her.

Flavia thoughtfully ruffled Scuto's fur. 'You know,'

she said presently, 'there's a mystery here. I think there's someone behind all these bad things that are happening.'

'Behind your father's shipwreck?'

'No. Behind Venalicius being set free and the bankers wanting to take our home.'

'Who?' said Nubia. 'Venalicius?'

'Maybe. I don't know. But I have a few ideas about how we could find out. What time did Pliny say he was sending the carruca to pick us up?'

'He said he would send it around noon,' said Jonathan.

'Then we only have a few hours. We'll have to work fast.'

'Uncle Gaius, can we go to the forum with you this morning?'

Flavia's uncle frowned at her as he tore a piece of bread from the disc-shaped loaf. The bailiffs' dawn visit had left him in a grim mood. 'Why?'

'We want to help,' said Flavia honestly.

He sighed. 'I don't think so, Flavia. I have to go to the barber's first and there's nothing for you to do there. And the bankers won't be impressed by two girls tugging the hem of my toga.'

'We won't be any trouble. Please can we come, Uncle Gaius? Nubia's good at seeing things and I'm good at getting ideas.'

Her uncle's face softened. 'Very well,' he said. 'But no toga-tugging.'

Not for the first time, Lupus stood beside Aristo in the office of Ostia's junior magistrate, Marcus Artorius Bato. This time Jonathan was with them, too. It was a small bright room with an arched window that over-looked the red-tiled roof of the temple of Venus next door. Lupus inhaled. Bato's office smelt of ink, wax, and papyrus, with a faint undertone of stale incense. Scrolls and wax tablets covered the large table and filled baskets underneath. In one corner was a small personal shrine to Hercules. The young magistrate tipped his chair back and eyed the trio with amusement in his pale eyes.

'These your bodyguards?' he asked Aristo.

'My pupils,' replied Aristo coolly. 'I'm giving them a lesson in Roman justice. Trying to explain how bailiffs can seize a shipwrecked captain's goods the day after he returns home.'

Bato scowled and let his chair fall forward. 'Oh, that. Captain Geminus obviously didn't read the codicil. Nasty business.'

'How do you know about it?' Aristo raised an eyebrow.

'My superior, Aulus Egrilius Rufus, mentioned it to me. But that has to do with bankers' contracts, not Roman law. Nor Roman justice.'

'I see. Then would Roman justice be allowing a known kidnapper and slave-dealer to be set free without trial?'

'Venalicius!' Bato almost spat the word out. 'That man is a disgusting, vile worm!'

Lupus grunted his agreement. He was beginning to like Bato.

'So how is it that a "vile, disgusting worm" is wandering around Ostia?' asked Aristo quietly.

'You tell me,' said Bato. 'What else could grease Rufus's palm enough to let that scum slip through his fingers?'

'Money?' said Aristo.

'Yes, and lots of it.' Bato leaned forward and lowered his voice. 'A heavy pouch full of gold convinced Rufus that Venalicius – we don't even know if that's his real name – could walk free until enough witnesses were brought to trial.'

'But there are plenty of witnesses that he kidnapped freeborn children!' cried Jonathan.

'Who?' Bato snorted. 'You?'

'Well . . . yes!'

'How old are you?'

'I was eleven last month,' said Jonathan.

'No good, I'm afraid. Witnesses can't be children or slaves. Only adult Roman citizens.'

'Pollius Felix!' cried Jonathan. 'The Patron. He's a

citizen. And a friend of the Emperor's. He'll testify. He was here in Ostia a few weeks ago.'

'By Hercules!' Bato slammed his fist onto the table and several papyrus scrolls rolled over the edge and onto the floor. 'Rufus told me Felix was out of the country. In Alexandria. This is bad. Very bad.'

Lupus scribbled something on his wax tablet and showed it to Aristo.

'Rufus,' said Aristo, reading Lupus's tablet. He looked up sharply at Bato. 'You said your superior is named Rufus. Is he related to the banker Rufus? Of Rufus and Dexter?'

Bato nodded and sighed. 'They're one and the same man.' He shook his head wearily. 'Never trust a banker turned politician.'

'Flavius Geminus!' The short man behind the banker's stall leapt to his feet, knocking an abacus onto a pile of silver coins. With his narrow face and long front teeth he reminded Flavia of a rat.

'Yes?' said Gaius. Flavia could see that her uncle was surprised to be recognised so far from home.

'We all heard you were shipwrecked and at the gates of Hades.'

'Oh,' said Gaius, and a look of realisation crossed his face. 'Oh, you think I'm –'

'Pater!' said Flavia loudly. And before her uncle could protest, 'Pater, imagine that! He thought you were practically dead. You know: very *weak and helpless* and at the gates of Hades. But you're not, are you *pater*?'

'Er . . . no! As you can see,' said Captain Geminus's twin brother, 'the reports of my condition were exaggerated . . . that is, you can see that I broke my nose when the boat crashed . . . er, I mean *ran aground* on some rocks but, but otherwise I feel fine. In fact, I feel like a new man.' He stood a little taller and brushed an invisible speck of lint from his toga.

'And . . .' He glanced at Flavia and she nodded back at him encouragingly. 'And what do you think you're doing? Threatening to take my home away! Sending your bailiffs at dawn, terrifying my . . . my daughter and the rest of the household!'

'I'm sorry, Captain Geminus,' said the rat-faced banker, recovering himself somewhat. 'But there's been a run on our reserves and we've been forced to call in our loans.' He licked his thin lips and glanced nervously round the forum, as if he were looking for someone to back him up.

'Great Neptune's beard!' Gaius banged his fist on the banker's table and caused the coins to jump. Beneath the table a watchdog began to bark.

'We're within our rights.' The banker took an involuntary step back and licked his lips again. 'Tell you what. I'll give you an extra week to come up with the money. But you still have to vacate the premises by sundown this evening and hand over the key. We don't want objects going missing.'

'Very well,' growled Gaius and started to turn away.

Flavia tugged her uncle's toga and when he bent down she whispered in his ear.

'Writing,' said Gaius, turning back. 'I want that in writing.'

The banker glared at Flavia. 'Very well,' he said between clenched teeth. 'I'll draw up a document now.'

As Flavia and her uncle watched the banker scribble his promise on a scrap of papyrus, Nubia heard a sound which made her skin crawl: the clink of chains. She slowly turned and looked out between the columns into the bright forum.

There. On a low wooden platform in the shadow of the great white temple across the forum. A dozen slaves, all chained at the neck just as she had once been.

Her hand went involuntarily to her throat and she left the cool shadows of the colonnade to cross the hot, open space. People began to move with her: sailors, merchants, soldiers, a few women. The slave-dealer had not yet announced the auction but the jingle of iron links could mean only one thing. Some of the people jostled her, but she felt none of them, saw none of them.

Nubia heard Flavia calling her name but her feet refused to stop. They took her across the forum.

Now the slave-dealer – a man she didn't recognise – was beginning to summon buyers. 'Step closer, Ostians! Examine the fine flesh on show today.'

Nubia stared.

She had been sold naked, but these men wore white loincloths.

She had been thin and covered with sores, these muscular young men were smooth and oiled.

She had not dared to raise her eyes in her shame. These men looked straight ahead, proudly – almost arrogantly – above the heads of the crowd.

The slave-dealer, a tall, dark-haired man in a toga, stepped onto the platform. 'Young men in their prime!' he called. 'They're not cheap but they're quality . . . Suitable to be trained as gladiators, bodyguards, litter-bearers . . . Each one has a reserve price of twenty-five thousand sestercii. Step up! Have a good look before the sale next week!'

Most of the chained men had olive skin and strong noses; Nubia guessed they were from Syria or Judaea. But two had skin as black as hers. And one of them, she saw as she finally arrived at the foot of the platform, one of them was her eldest brother Taharqo.

SCROLL VIII

Lupus's thoughts were as tangled as seaweed in a net, but the deep blue interior of the carruca had begun to calm him. The carriage Pliny had sent for them had a cedar frame covered with blue silk curtains. These curtains were drawn against the hot noonday sun and created a deep blue light which filled the interior of the carriage, flickering gently as shadows and sunlight passed overhead. It was almost like being underwater, thought Lupus.

Captain Geminus lay on the cushioned bench which ran along the left-hand side of the carruca. The rocking motion of the well-sprung carriage had put him to sleep, so the others spoke in low tones.

Lupus sat forward and listened to Nubia. She was telling them how she had seen her older brother in the slave-market.

'Are you sure it was your brother?' Jonathan asked her in a whisper.

Nubia nodded. In the blue light her lemon-yellow tunic looked green.

'Did someone buy him?' asked Miriam softly.

Nubia shook her head and Flavia explained, 'The auction's not until the Ides, in three days.' Flavia had perched beside her father to make sure he didn't slip off the bench.

'Did your brother recognise you, Nubia?' asked Aristo.

'Alas! I do not think so.' Nubia hung her head. 'The slave-seller had the whip.'

'If the slaves don't keep their eyes straight ahead,' explained Flavia, 'then he whips them.'

'Maybe we could buy your brother and set him free!' suggested Jonathan in an excited whisper.

'They're starting the bidding at twenty-five thousand sestercii,' said Flavia, and added: 'Each.'

'Oh.'

Flavia looked at Aristo. 'What did you find out at the magistrate's? Is it true the bailiff can take our house?'

Aristo leaned forward, and kept his voice low. 'I'm afraid your father didn't read the whole contract when he borrowed the money. He didn't read the part in small writing at the end: the codicil.'

'Oh,' said Flavia, and glanced down at her father's thin face. 'He's not very good at that sort of thing.'

'I usually advise him, but this time he didn't consult me,' said Aristo. 'He can be a bit impetuous.'

Flavia gave him a rueful smile. 'It runs in the family,' she said.

Lupus showed Jonathan his wax tablet.

Jonathan nodded and turned to Flavia. 'Bato also told us why they let Venalicius go.'

'Why?'

'He bribed them.'

Aristo explained: 'They claim there are no witnesses. Venalicius gave the chief magistrate Aulus Egrilius Rufus an amount of money to let him go until they can find enough witnesses for the trial. If he runs away, he forfeits the money.'

'Rufus!' cried Flavia, and then covered her mouth with her hand as her father stirred. 'Rufus?' she said again. 'He's one of the bankers who wants to take our house away!'

'We know,' said Jonathan. 'Was he the one you saw at the forum today?'

'No,' said Flavia. 'That was Dexter. He's horrible. He has a face like a rat.'

'And he has big watchdog,' added Nubia.

'Did he say why they were being so mean to your father?' said Jonathan.

'He said they didn't have any money or reserves or something . . . but wait! You just said Venalicius gave them a huge bribe to let him out until the trial. So they were lying when they said they didn't have any money.'

'Either that or their debts are so big that even Venalicius' bribe wasn't enough to cover them,' suggested Aristo.

'Oh,' moaned Flavia. 'My head hurts just thinking about it. And I feel a bit sick.'

'Me, too,' said Jonathan. 'It's bumpier now. I think we've left the main road. Can you open the curtains, Lupus? The ties are by you.'

Lupus scowled. He liked the underwater effect caused by the sun shining through the blue silk. It helped him think. And he needed to think up a way to raise one hundred thousand sestercii.

'Lupus,' hissed Flavia. 'Please open the curtains.'

Reluctantly, Lupus untied one panel of the filmy fabric and pulled it back. Behind him was the sea, glittering in the hot October sun. A faint breeze filled the interior and caused the silk walls to balloon.

'Oh, that's better.' Jonathan burped gently.

'Behold!' said Nubia and pointed to a butter-coloured villa further along the coast, just visible through some pines. 'House of Pliny.'

Lupus sighed. There was no way he could ever come up with one hundred thousand sestercii. And without that money it would be very difficult for him to fulfil his vow to take revenge on Venalicius.

Difficult, but not impossible.

Nubia had been to Pliny's Laurentum villa once before. A few months earlier, the four friends had helped rescue its previous owner, Admiral Pliny. On that occasion the old man had invited them to dine in his triclinium overlooking the sea.

It was in this same triclinium that they now settled down to eat. The serving girls had put linen dining-slippers on their feet and poured water over their hands. As the sun began its dazzling descent, they waited for the slaves to bring in the first course.

Nubia gazed around the room. On three sides, spiral columns of pink marble framed the sparkling sea. The columns rose from a low marble wall about as high as her waist. Beyond this sparkling white parapet was a dizzy drop to the rocks and sea below. On the remaining side of the triclinium, two green pillars flanked a tunnel of sunny and shaded courtyards which stretched all the way back to the double doors through which they had entered.

Nubia's eyes kept returning to an object in the dining-room that had not been there before. Against one of the green marble columns stood a life-sized statue of the hero Perseus.

The story of Perseus was one of the first myths Nubia had ever heard. Later she learned that heroes in Greek and Roman stories were always having to go on long journeys, usually to defeat a monster and bring back something as proof.

Perseus had to bring back the head of a creature named Medusa. Once she had been a beautiful woman, but she had boasted of her beauty to the gods. As a punishment, they had made her so hideous that anyone who looked at her turned to stone. Perseus avoided her terrible gaze by using his shield as a mirror, and cut off her head without looking directly at her.

The bronze statue in Pliny's triclinium showed the moment after the deed. Perseus, his handsome face averted, was holding up his gory trophy. Medusa was shown with her mouth open in a silent scream of rage and her snaky hair writhing as if still alive. From the hero's left arm hung a shield, round and curiously flat. Nubia looked closer. The shield was coated with a thin layer of silver, polished to mirror brightness.

Pliny noticed her gaze. 'My uncle loved beautiful things,' he said. 'That statue is one of his most recent purchases.'

Jonathan narrowed his eyes at it. 'Isn't it a bit . . . gaudy?'

'It's Hellenistic,' explained Pliny. 'The Hellenistic Greeks adored the overly dramatic. It's not particularly to my taste, either.'

Pliny reclined beside Miriam on the central couch. Flavia's father lay on the couch to his right, propped up with several cushions. Occupying his own couch on the left, Aristo rarely took his eyes off Pliny and Miriam.

The slave-girls were serving the appetisers now: prawns glazed with honey and cumin. Nubia took one from the dish and ate it thoughtfully. She wondered why Pliny kept glancing at the shield on the statue.

Suddenly she had the answer: he could see Miriam's face reflected in its mirror-like surface. Pliny had a double view of Miriam: her profile as well as her front view.

'I'm only here for another week or so,' Pliny was saying, 'then it's back up to Rome, where I'm studying to be a lawyer.' He looked away from the shield and glanced round at them all. 'But I wanted to make notes about my uncle's last hours while it was still fresh in my mind. I'm a historian, too, you see. And architect; I'm designing an extension to this villa.' He dabbed the corner of his mouth with his napkin. 'I've already drawn up my own plans,' he added, and glanced at Miriam. 'Would you like to see them?'

Without taking her eyes from her plate, Miriam nodded politely.

'*I'd* like to see your plans,' said Jonathan, sucking some honey sauce from his fingers. 'I design things, too.'

Pliny nodded at Jonathan. 'I'll show you tomorrow.'

'Delicious,' said Marcus from his couch. 'Those were delicious prawns. It's good to be back in civilisation.'

'Thank you, Captain Geminus. They're very fresh. One of the local fishermen caught them just this morning.' Pliny smiled at Flavia's father. 'Tell me, are you feeling better?'

'Much better, thank you.'

'After dinner I usually have one of my freedmen read to me from one of the classics. But your experience must rival that of Odysseus . . . will you tell us how you were shipwrecked?'

'Yes!' cried Flavia. 'You said you'd tell us when you felt stronger.'

'Only if you don't mind,' said Pliny.

'Not at all,' said Flavia's father. 'Though I am hardly Odysseus.' He lay back on his cushions.

'I believe the volcano caused the wreck, though we didn't know it at the time. It was the last week of August, and we had left the port of Alexandria the day before, having taken on a full cargo of spices. We were making the run to Crete. That's the most dangerous part of the voyage because it's across open water.

'Suddenly, without warning, an enormous wave was upon us. At one point it was no further than you are from me.' He looked up at them with something like awe in his expression. 'It was like a cliff of green glass and I could see fish swimming in it above my ship.' He paused for a moment, shaking his head.

'There was no time to tack. The wall of water struck the *Myrtilla* amidships. It was terrifying. One moment my ship was beneath us, the next she was gone. Thank Jupiter my crew and I were all on deck.

We found ourselves floating among flotsam and managed to cling to bits of timber.'

His eyes filled with tears. 'In only one respect am I like Odysseus,' he said quietly. 'I lost all my men. When it grew light again, they were gone.' For a moment he was silent.

'After a day or two,' he continued presently, 'I was washed up onto a rocky island inhabited only by birds. I survived for a few weeks by killing the birds and eating them raw.'

Nubia tried not to shudder.

'I must have become delirious,' said Captain Geminus, 'because the next thing I remember is lying in the bottom of a Cretan fishing boat. A few days later we met a Syrian merchant ship on its way from Rhodes to Rome. The fishermen persuaded them to take me aboard. The Syrians let me sleep in the galley. They lived on a meagre diet of porridge, but they shared what they had with me. There was nobody willing to attend to my wounds and we made slow progress because many harbours were damaged by the earthquake and the wave. We finally reached Ostia a few days ago.'

'Surely the gods were watching over you,' said Pliny.

'Yes.' Flavia's father stared up at the high blue plaster ceiling of the dining-room. Patterns of light reflected from the sea outside flickered across its surface. 'I pray that some of my crew survived. But my ship and its cargo of spices lies at the bottom of the sea. There's no doubt of that.'

Nobody spoke for a long time.

'My entire fortune was invested in those spices,' added Flavia's father. 'If only I could recover it!'

Pliny nodded gravely. 'If we could bring up just a fraction of the treasure that lies beneath the sea then we would be rich beyond our dreams.' He chewed his last prawn thoughtfully. 'There's even a wreck here at Laurentum. They say the ship was carrying casks of gold and the weight of the treasure sank it.'

'Here?' said Flavia, her eyes bright with interest. 'A sunken treasure near here?'

Pliny nodded. 'Just there. Do you see those rocks? The ones with the cormorants on them? The birds drying their wings?'

They all nodded and Nubia shaded her eyes with her hand.

Lupus pushed back his chair with a scrape of iron on marble and ran to the low parapet that surrounded the triclinium.

'When the water is clear you can see the wreck lying there, seemingly within your grasp. But it's an illusion.'

'Why doesn't someone dive down and get it?' asked Flavia, pushing her own chair back and standing up.

'The water is deeper than it looks,' said Pliny.

'Several local fishermen have tried. As far as I know, the only one to reach the wreck never came back up. According to the peasants round here, a terrible monster guards the treasure.'

'Oh.' Flavia slowly sat down again.

The serving-girls were bringing in the main course – fried veal in a raisin and cream sauce – so Lupus returned to the table. As he sat down Nubia glanced over at him. She saw a curious look in his eyes.

Triumph.

SCROLL IX

Flavia rubbed her teeth with her tooth stick and studied the mosaic seahorse on the floor. She and her friends had been given small but attractive rooms around a green courtyard near the sea-view triclinium. Each room had a different sea creature on the black and white mosaic floor.

Flavia sipped some water from a small jug and rinsed her mouth, then swallowed. 'I wonder if there is such a thing as a seahorse,' she said to Nubia, who was sitting on the bed with Nipur, searching for ticks in his fur.

'We have a dolphin on our floor,' said Jonathan. He and Lupus stood in the doorway. 'And Aristo has a crayfish.'

'It's a beautiful villa,' sighed Flavia.

'Lupus has something exciting to tell us,' said Jonathan.

Flavia looked at the younger boy with interest. Lupus's sea-green eyes were bright as he held up his wax tablet.

I CAN DIVE

'You can dive?' Flavia frowned. Then her eyes widened. 'In the sea?'

Lupus nodded and added another word with his stylus.

I CAN DIVE DEEP

'Deep enough to reach maybe some treasure?'

Lupus nodded.

'How?' said Nubia. 'Fishermen couldn't do it. How can you?'

I USED TO DIVE FOR SPONGES

'You did?' Jonathan stared at Lupus. 'You never told us you were a sponge diver.'

A shadow flickered across Lupus's eyes and he wrote:

MY FATHER WAS A SPONGE DIVER

'Oh,' they said.

Then Flavia asked a question none of them had dared to ask before.

'Lupus. You told us once that your parents were dead. Were they murdered?'

Lupus scowled and gave an impatient nod.

Then he underlined the first sentence he had written and held up his tablet:

I CAN DIVE DEEP

Flavia turned to the others. 'Do you realise what this means?' she whispered. 'If we could bring up even one chest of that gold, then I could pay father's debts. Maybe even buy him a new ship.'

'And I could give your uncle enough money to buy a house with a garden,' said Jonathan, 'so he could marry my sister.'

'I could buy my brother from slave-market,' said Nubia, her amber eyes bright with hope. 'And set him free!'

Flavia turned to Lupus. 'What about you, Lupus?' she asked. 'What would you buy if we get the sunken treasure?'

He etched one word on the tablet and showed it to them:

REVENGE

*

'What on earth is wrong with all of you this morning?' scowled Aristo. 'Jonathan confused Scylla with Charybdis, Flavia's sums are off by a mile and you've completely forgotten your Greek vocabulary. Well, all except for you, Lupus. Even you seem distracted, Nubia.'

'We're all thinking about the treasure,' said Flavia.

Aristo sighed. 'Flavia. You heard what Pliny said at dinner last night. There's no way we can dive that deep.'

'But Lupus is a spongy diver,' said Nubia.

'What?'

'Lupus used to dive for sponges,' said Flavia, hopping up and down in her chair.

'No. I'm sorry. I don't believe it.' Aristo folded his arms. 'There are very few places around here where sponges grow.'

Lupus stared back at him for a moment. Then he wrote on his wax tablet, pressing so hard that the stylus crunched the wood beneath.

I'M NOT FROM HERE!

'No?' said Aristo. 'Then why don't you tell us where you're from?'

Lupus wrote on his tablet and held it up. He had written a word in Greek.

ΣΥΜΙ

'What?' said Flavia, snatching the table and peering at it. 'SYMI? What's a Symi?'

Aristo said something to Lupus in Greek and Lupus folded his own arms and nodded.

'I don't believe it,' repeated Aristo.

'What?' they all cried.

'He's Greek. Lupus is Greek.'

'You're Greek?' Jonathan asked Lupus in disbelief.

Lupus nodded.

Aristo slowly unfolded his arms. 'And you used to dive for sponges on the island of Symi?'

'His father is spongy diver, too,' said Nubia.

'That actually explains a lot,' said Aristo.

'So Lupus can dive for the treasure,' said Flavia. 'And all our problems will be solved!'

Aristo leaned forward, resting his elbows on the cool marble surface of the table. 'Lupus. Do you really think you can reach depths a strong young fisherman couldn't?'

Lupus nodded emphatically.

'Well, then . . .' Aristo leaned back. 'That would benefit us all. If we could pay off Captain Geminus's debts . . .'

'So can we cancel today's lesson?' asked Jonathan eagerly.

'Not cancel . . .' Aristo's brown eyes gleamed, '. . . so much as modify. Flavia, you could do some research on wrecks and salvage. Maybe Jonathan can help me design some equipment to lift the treasure chests, if Lupus really *can* dive that deep. And we should investigate the wreck right away. But first we'd better ask Pliny's permission.'

They told Pliny as soon as he returned from his morning walk.

'By Hercules!' said the young man. 'What an excellent idea! We'll split any treasure you find. I can supply you with a rowing boat and I'll put one of my people at your disposal. How's that?'

'Excellent,' said Aristo. 'We should get started immediately, while the weather lasts. It's almost the Ides of October. This fair weather could change any day.'

'I'll get someone to show you where the boats and fishing tackle are kept,' said Pliny. He clapped his hands and when a boy in red appeared he said, 'Ask our new freedman to join us.'

'Yes, master.'

A few minutes later a handsome young man in a red tunic came into the room. He had dark hair and eyes and wore a soft cone-shaped hat on his head. When he saw Flavia and her friends his face brightened.

'Phrixus!' Flavia cried. 'How are you?'

'Free, Miss Flavia.' He pointed to the hat on his head. 'Young master Pliny gave me my freedom yesterday morning. I'm a citizen now and my new name is Gaius Plinius Phrixus.'

Pliny's eyes sparkled and he turned to Flavia. 'After you told me of his bravery and of his devotion to my uncle . . . well, I could scarcely do anything else!'

'Congratulations, Phrixus!' they all cried.

Phrixus nodded and smiled at them, but Flavia saw there were still shadows of grief beneath his eyes.

'How are you, Jonathan?' asked Phrixus as he led them out of the sea-view triclinium across a bright, sheltered terrace. A dozen terracotta flowerpots filled the hot air with the scent of violets and the buzz of bees.

'I'm well now, thank you.'

Phrixus opened a gate in the yellow plaster-covered wall and the dogs jostled through it in front of them.

'You suffer from asthma like my master, but you lived,' Phrixus said quietly as he led them down some sandy wooden steps towards the beach.

'I almost didn't,' said Jonathan.

'Jonathan was unconscious for three days,' Flavia told Phrixus.

'Did you go back to the Pliny?' asked Nubia as they reached the level beach. 'I mean, the old Pliny?'

Phrixus nodded and they all stopped as he turned to them. 'Tascius and I found his body two days after the eruption. He was lying on the sailcloth, just where we left him on that dreadful night. He looked so peaceful, as if he were sleeping.'

The young freedman turned and moved quickly

across the dunes. His conical hat blew off and Jonathan picked it up and dusted the sand off and ran to catch up with him.

Phrixus took the hat with a grunt of thanks and pushed it under his belt. He was heading towards a boathouse set into the low sandy cliffs near the shore. Further along and set back from the boathouse was a dense row of mulberry trees. Jonathan could just make out the red roof-tiles of a neighbouring villa through the leaves.

The dogs came running up from the water to join them, then surged ahead as they saw where everyone was going. Jonathan and his friends followed them into the dim interior of the boathouse, a brick vault built into the sandy cliff.

The dogs ran back and forth, noses down and tails wagging, delighted to discover such new and unusual scents. In the cool gloom of the vaulted space, Jonathan inhaled deeply. The boathouse had a musty perfume all its own: briny wood, pine-pitch and canvas, with undertones of kelp, mould and candle wax.

Jonathan liked it. As his eyes grew accustomed to the gloom, he saw several small boats in various states of disrepair on the sandy floor of the boathouse. And ranged along the inward curving wall were many other interesting objects.

As the others helped Phrixus push the biggest boat

out of the gloom into the bright sunshine, Jonathan and the dogs investigated these other items. He had not brought his wax tablet, so he made a conscious effort to memorise them, using a method his father had taught him:

one small rowing boat (good condition)
one medium rowing boat (hole in stern)
one half-built rowing boat, still on its frame
useful planks of wood
several coils of rope
three oak buckets (one filled with assorted fishing
    hooks, some quite big)
seven fishing nets
twelve cork floats
an old sailcloth
a small iron anchor (rusted)
a broken trident (middle prong missing)
four old oars (different sizes)

Presently Jonathan was aware of Flavia calling him from the beach and he came squinting back out into the bright sunshine, followed by the dogs. Although it was October and there was still a haze of volcanic ash in the air, the midday sun was hot.

The others were pushing a sky-blue fishing boat into the water, and its keel rasped on pebbly sand until it bobbed on the water. Phrixus and Aristo jumped into the boat. They took Tigris and Nipur, and after some manoeuvring the young Greeks lifted Scuto aboard, too. The four friends clambered in after the dogs.

Most of Jonathan's cream-coloured tunic was soaking wet but he didn't mind: it cooled him off.

Ball in mouth, Scuto sat in the bows as lookout. Tigris and Nipur ran from one side of the boat to the other, making it rock.

'Stop it, Tigris,' said Jonathan. 'You, too, Nipur. You're making me feel seasick.'

Aristo laughed. His face was shining. 'My family used to have a boat,' he said, 'before Fortuna abandoned us.'

The puppies settled down as Aristo took one oar and Phrixus took the other. Soon the boat was moving out to sea, heading for the rocky island with the cormorants. The water was calm with a dusty skin on its surface, and as the young men pulled on the oars, the boat surged ahead with a quick rustle of water, like a knife cutting green silk.

Jonathan closed his eyes for a moment. He could feel the living motion of the boat and the sun hot on his head and shoulders. His tunic was nearly dry.

'Pliny's villa looks so beautiful from here.' Flavia's voice.

Jonathan opened his eyes and twisted round.

The butter-yellow villa on the shore stood out

against the dark green woods behind it. He could see its columns and arches and red-tiled roof, its sea-view triclinium and the square tower rising at one end of the complex. The highest floor of this tower had large arched windows which let the sky show through like a tile of blue turquoise. As he looked, he saw the dark shape of a distant figure step into one of these blue spaces.

'I see the Pliny,' said Nubia, who had the sharpest eyes of all of them. She waved and they saw the figure wave back.

'Who's that with him?' said Flavia, and Jonathan saw the silhouette of a second figure join the first.

'It's Miriam,' said Aristo, and his jaw clenched as he pulled on the oar.

Presently they stopped rowing and Phrixus stood up in the boat.

'I came out here with the admiral once,' said Phrixus. His handsome face gleamed with sweat and there were patches of damp on the armpits of his red tunic. 'We discovered that if you position the boat in a direct line between the tower and Cormorant Island and those three umbrella pines on the promontory . . .' he peered down into the water and pointed in triumph, '. . . you will find the wreck!'

'Careful!' cried Jonathan. The boat had tipped alarmingly as his three friends and Scuto all eagerly leaned over the port side.

'I can't see anything!' said Flavia.

Lupus grunted and pointed. He had stripped down to his loincloth and his back next to Jonathan was smooth and hot and brown.

'I think I am seeing the boat,' said Nubia.

'It's down deep,' said Phrixus. 'The water isn't as clear as it usually is. You can see it as a dark shape against the sandy bottom.'

Jonathan gazed down into the water. It was clearer than the water had been off the coast of Surrentum but he still couldn't see anything that looked like a wreck. Beside him, Lupus scooped up a handful of seawater and wet the back of his neck. Then with two handfuls he splashed his face. He took several short panting breaths, followed by a long deep one. Jonathan could actually see his ribcage expand when he inhaled.

Finally, Lupus opened his wax tablet and scribbled something on it. Then he handed it to Jonathan.

PRAY AGAINST SHARKS!

With that, he was over the side, as smoothly as an eel from a fisherman's bucket. He made barely a splash.

'How will he breathe?' cried Nubia.

'He won't,' said Aristo. 'He'll hold his breath.'

Jonathan watched his friend sink deeper and deeper.

And suddenly he saw the wreck. He hadn't seen it because it was so deep. He looked at the others and shook his head.

'It's too far down,' said Jonathan. 'He'll never reach it.'

Lupus felt the weight of the water resist him from below and push him from above. Using his arms and legs, he propelled himself down from green to blue to darker blue. It was the slowest way to descend, but this was just a practice dive. Later he would use his special sponge-diving techniques for a quick descent.

The wreck was very deep, so he set himself the goal of just touching it. The pressure in his head was growing, so he pinched his nose and gently blew.

Presently he felt the desire to breathe. But he was not even halfway there. He was badly out of practice.

Still, he had set himself a goal and he would achieve it. Down and down he went, kicking and pulling at the water with his arms. Deeper and deeper into the blue depths.

Nubia let out her breath in a gasp and sucked in a lungful of air. Flavia realised she'd been holding her breath in sympathy with Lupus. He must be desperate to breathe by now. The three friends exchanged anxious looks and bent further over the side.

'There!' said Flavia. 'I think I see him coming up. Or is it? It looks too small . . .' Suddenly she screamed.

A severed head bobbed like a ball on the surface of the water.

SCROLL X

Nubia leaned over the side of the boat, stretched out her hands and lifted the dripping object from the water.

It was the carved wooden head of a woman. It still bore traces of paint: red on the parted lips and black on the eyes which stared blankly over Nubia's shoulder, like a soothsayer gazing into the future.

'It must be part of the ship's figurehead,' said Aristo.

Suddenly there was an explosion of spray and Lupus was gasping in the water before them.

'Lupus!' they cried.

Aristo held out his hand and pulled Lupus up into the boat. Lupus grinned at them, pushed back his dripping hair and reached for his wax tablet.

'You did it,' said Phrixus. 'You reached the ship. That's amazing. Very few of the local fishermen can dive that deep.'

Lupus wrote on his tablet.

FRONT OF SHIP LOWEST

Then he added something

THINK I SAW CRACK IN HULL

'Did you go inside?' asked Flavia. 'Did you see the treasure?'

Lupus shook his head and wrote

OUT OF PRACTICE. HAVE TO TRAIN.

Nubia frowned. 'How do you train?'

Lupus sucked in a big breath and flicked his fingers up, one after the other, starting with the little finger of his left hand. When all ten were up he started again on the next beat. Jonathan caught on and started to count:

'. . . twelve, thirteen, fourteen, fifteen . . .'

Nubia and Flavia joined in.

They had reached one hundred by the time Lupus opened his mouth to suck in a lungful of air.

After that, Lupus's three friends took turns diving to see if they could reach the wreck, too. But the water was colder at this depth and its chill made Jonathan wheeze and Nubia shiver. Flavia was still the weakest swimmer of the four. The feel of the water closing over her head made her panic. She also found it impossible to keep her eyes open under water. It didn't seem natural.

'You'd better be the one who dives, Lupus,' she said

through chattering teeth, as she towelled off. 'And we'll help you all we can.'

'What can we do?' Jonathan asked.

Lupus flipped open his wax tablet.

I NEED ROPE he wrote

AND BIG FLAT HEAVY ROCKS

AND MAYBE FISHNET

'I saw rope and fishing net in the boathouse,' said Jonathan.

'And there are rocks further up the shore,' added Phrixus. He squinted up into the turquoise sky. 'But it's already well past noon. I suggest we have lunch and then get everything prepared for a proper dive tomorrow. Will that give you enough time to train?' he asked Lupus.

Lupus nodded and wrote:

I HOPE SO. I WANT THAT TREASURE.

*

Lupus leapt out of the boat first and waded through the waves towards young Pliny, who was hurrying down the beach with Miriam. The two of them were shaded by her papyrus parasol. Scuto and the puppies splashed into the water after Lupus, then ran barking back and forth between the converging groups.

Lupus held up his dripping prize.

'By Hercules!' exclaimed Pliny, his dark eyes bright with pleasure. 'You've recovered the head of the goddess. May I keep it?'

Lupus nodded and Pliny took the head.

'Aphrodite, the foam-born,' said Pliny softly. 'Venus emerges from the sea and comes to Laurentum.' He slapped Lupus's back. 'Thank you, Lupus. I must confess, I didn't think you could do it. But you're a real urinator!'

'He's a *what*?' said Flavia, out of breath.

Pliny laughed at the expression on their faces. 'Urinator. It means "diver". We should celebrate.'

'But we didn't get the treasure,' said Jonathan. 'Lupus only barely reached the wreck.'

'He has to train himself to hold his breath for even longer,' added Flavia, pulling the towel around her shoulders.

'Phrixus and I are going to adapt the boat for diving,' said Jonathan.

Nubia added, 'Aristo and I are looking for heavy stones on the beach this afternoon.'

'And I,' announced Flavia, 'am going to research the dangers of the deep. Can I use your uncle's library?'

'Of course,' said Pliny. 'It's close to your room.' He

put the figurehead under his left arm and joined Miriam beneath the shade of her papyrus parasol again, touching her elbow lightly to direct her back up towards the villa. Suddenly he stopped and turned to look at them. 'How would you all like to have a banquet on the beach this evening, to celebrate Lupus's success?'

They all nodded, especially Lupus.

'Good.' Pliny glanced at Miriam. 'Tonight is the Meditrinalia, when we drink the new wine mixed with the old and thank the gods for their provision. Several years ago my uncle and I celebrated the feast down on the beach. It will be just like old times. I'll tell the kitchen slaves to slaughter a pig at once.'

It was autumn, the time of year when the hours of daylight grow shorter. And so it was almost dark by the time they finished their supper of spit-roasted pig, flat bread and chickpea stew. The sun had set and the sky was filled with a blue so vibrant that it seemed to sing. The sea was black and the embers of the fire glowed red.

As a pretty slave-girl named Thelma handed out fig-cakes, Phrixus appeared and set a beautiful Greek mixing-bowl on the sand. The krater had red figures of the wine-god Dionysus and his female followers dancing across the surface. Pliny rose from his reclining position and took two silver jugs. From one he poured a stream of wine into the krater. It gleamed ruby red in the firelight.

'This is last year's wine,' he explained with a smile. Then he emptied the other jug into the big krater. This wine was so dark it was almost black. 'And this,' he said, 'is the new.'

Flavia peered into the krater and watched the two colours mix. Then she settled down onto her stomach in the soft sand, rested her chin on her hands and gazed at the handsome god Dionysus. On this vase he was shown bearded, with his head thrown back in joy.

Pliny bent and dipped a flat silver bowl – a patera – in the krater. Then he tipped the patera, and a stream of red wine spattered onto the sand.

'*Novum vetus vinum bibo,*' he recited, '*novo veteri morbo medeor.* I drink new and old wine, and am healed of new and old disease.' He dipped one of the jugs into the mixing-bowl, poured the blend of new and old into a small silver cup, and handed it to Flavia. She rose up onto her knees to accept it. Pliny nodded her towards her father. 'Captain Geminus,' he said, 'to you the first mixed wine of the Meditrinalia.'

Still on her knees, Flavia shuffled over the sand, holding the cup carefully out before her. Her father was propped up on a cushioned litter. Even though it was a mild night, he had a blanket around his thin body.

As he leaned forward, Flavia supported the back of

his neck with her left hand and held the cup to his lips with her right.

'Thank you, my little owl.' He wiped a dribble of red wine from the corner of his mouth and leaned back against the cushions.

Meanwhile Pliny had filled other wine cups and Thelma was taking the blended wine round to the others, who sat or reclined on old carpets spread over the sand.

Presently, Phrixus and Thelma went back to the villa and Pliny sat down near Miriam. He sipped his wine and made a face. 'On the Meditrinalia the wine is supposed to have beneficial effects,' he said. 'But today it's more like the worst kind of medicine. It's been a terrible harvest.'

'It's not too bad,' said Captain Geminus. 'And it was a wonderful meal.'

'Would you like another fig-cake, pater?' asked Flavia.

Her father shook his head and closed his eyes. 'I wish I had more energy,' he murmured. 'I slept all day and yet I still feel tired.'

'Sleep is one of the best healers,' said Miriam, leaning over to pull the light blanket up around his shoulders. 'That's why my father wanted you to get away from Ostia. So you could rest and sleep. Then your body can heal itself.'

Captain Geminus nodded, his eyes still closed.

Flavia smoothed his hair from his forehead, struck again by how frail he looked.

'Play something nice, please, Nubia,' whispered Flavia. 'Something to help pater sleep.'

Nubia smiled and nodded. She took out the flute she wore on a cord around her neck and after a moment she played the 'Sailing Song'. Soon Lupus found the beat on a piece of driftwood with his spoon.

Flavia saw that both Aristo and Pliny were watching Miriam as they sipped their wine. She had closed her eyes and tipped her head back. Her long white tunic and her arms and throat looked pink in the red light of the coals.

As the last notes died away, a figure emerged from the darkness: Phrixus. He pushed seven torches into the soft sand around them. When the torches were lit, a golden circle of light surrounded the young diners.

'Phrixus,' said Pliny, as the freedman turned to go. 'Will you bring my lyre down to the beach?' He turned to the boys. 'You brought instruments, too, didn't you?'

Jonathan nodded. 'My barbiton and Lupus's drums. They're in our room.'

'And a tambourine please, Phrixus!' Flavia called out.

Phrixus was back with Thelma a few minutes later. They stepped into the circle of flickering torchlight and handed out the instruments, then vanished discreetly back into the darkness.

Pliny took the lyre in his left hand and fitted it against his left shoulder. Using a small ivory wand, he strummed some chords with his right hand.

'I don't have a very good singing voice,' he said, with a shy glance at Miriam. 'But I would like to sing for you, too. This is part of a Greek epic I composed when I was fourteen years old. I set it to music myself.'

SCROLL XI

Pliny cleared his throat and began to sing in Greek. It was a rather formal song and Nubia noticed he did not seem able to sing and strum at the same time. Once or twice she could tell he'd hit a slightly wrong note. But when he finished everyone clapped politely. Pliny bowed his head.

'A dithyramb!' Aristo's curls gleamed like copper in the firelight as he nodded. 'Very good.'

'Thank you.'

'I lost my own lyre in the eruption,' said Aristo, holding out his hand. 'May I?'

'Of course.' Pliny passed his instrument to Aristo, then held out the ivory wand.

'No thank you,' said Aristo. 'I just use my fingers.'

For a few moments the young Greek made some minor adjustments to the tuning. Then he turned to Nubia.

'Shall we play "Slave Song"?'

Nubia nodded and put the flute to her lips. She and Aristo looked at each other and began at precisely the same moment. Nubia had composed the song herself.

It had no words, but the image which had inspired it was that of a slave-girl sitting on the back of a camel, travelling in a caravan towards an oasis. Lupus drummed a steady beat, which Jonathan echoed with the low notes of his barbiton and Flavia with the muted jingle of her tambourine.

They finished softly and when the last notes died away there was no applause, just the crackling of the torches and the sighing of waves on the beach. Miriam's cheeks were wet and she wiped them with her fingers.

'Remarkable,' said Pliny at last. There was a strange catch in his voice. 'I have never heard anything like that. I remember now. My uncle spoke about you. I didn't make the connection before. Nubia, you are an exceptional musician. So are you, Aristo.'

Pliny stood and they all looked up at him. He was wearing a spotless cream tunic, with a broad purple stripe on each side. Flavia noticed he had trimmed his brown hair. The new haircut made his head look quite round.

'Excuse me,' he said. 'My hands. They're a bit sticky from the fig-cakes. I'm just going to rinse them.'

He moved quickly out of the circle of torchlight and down to the water.

Scuto ambled after him, tail wagging slowly. After a moment Flavia put down her tambourine and followed him, too.

For a few moments the three of them stood side by side on the shore and stared out over the water. Scuto raised his nose to test the sea breeze. The night was moonless and very dark apart from the breathtaking sweep of a hundred million stars blazing overhead.

It occurred to Flavia that it hadn't really been fair of Aristo to play the 'Slave Song' after Pliny's stiff dithyramb. Especially with all of them playing, too. But Pliny had been gracious in defeat.

'That was a very nice dinner,' Flavia said at last. 'Thank you for arranging it. And for having us all to stay.'

Pliny glanced sideways at her and she saw his eyes gleam wetly in the starlight. 'That's kind of you,' he said. For a moment she thought he was going to say something else. But he merely repeated, 'That's kind of you.'

Flavia bent to rinse her hands in a salty wave.

'Oh!' she cried. A greenish light fizzed in the water as she swished her hand.

'What?' Nubia had come up quietly behind them.

'Look!' breathed Flavia. As she pulled her hand through the black water it left a trail of greenish-yellow light which immediately faded. Scuto growled.

'Phosphorescence,' said Pliny. 'Nobody knows what causes it, but on dark nights the sea often burns with cold fire. It's harmless – or so my uncle told me.'

95

'Fox fur essence?' repeated Nubia, with a frown.

'Everybody! Come quickly!' called Flavia. The others – except for Flavia's father – rose and moved down to the water.

'Look!' said Flavia. She drew her hand through the water again and showed them the glowing trail her hand made.

Behind them, Lupus uttered a whoop, stripped off his tunic and ran splashing into the inky sea.

The black water shimmered yellow-green as he churned it with his hands and the drops he threw at them were like wet emeralds, fading even as they fell. Nubia laughed and walked into the water, too, looking behind her to see the brief trails of green light her legs made in the black water. The dogs barked at this strange behaviour.

It was a mild night and the water was deliciously warm. Soon all four friends were swimming and splashing in the shallow water.

When they swam, they left trails of fizzing light, and when they stood on the sandy sea bed to splash each other, the phosphorescence lit their laughing faces pale green.

Presently Lupus struck out into deeper water and turned on his back. It was a trick he had been trying to teach the others: to float on the water as if it were a supporting mattress.

'How do you do that?' asked Flavia in frustration,

watching as the other three floated on the silky surface of the water.

'Just relax,' Jonathan's voice came from her right. 'Make your hands like fans, with the fingers together, and keep them moving just a little.'

Flavia lay back and tried to relax, but water suddenly filled her mouth and she coughed.

'You might want to keep your mouth closed,' suggested Jonathan.

Flavia tried again. And again. At last, just as she was about to give up, she realised she was floating. Her hands had found the right motion.

Lupus was showing off, spitting a stream of water up from his mouth as if he were a spouting killer whale. The jet of water glowed yellow-green for a brief instant.

Flavia carefully turned her head and looked to her left, towards the shore. Miriam and the two young men were walking back up to join Flavia's father.

Just inside the circle of torchlight the puppies were wrestling. But Scuto remained close to the water, an alert shape silhouetted against the fire, watching to make sure no harm came to his mistress. Flavia smiled to herself and idly wondered what harm could possibly come to her here in this magical cove on such a glorious night.

At that very moment she felt the water push against her back, as if something had swum beneath her.

'What was that?' Jonathan's voice in the darkness sounded alarmed.

And then Nubia's trembling voice:

'Something touch me. Something big!'

SCROLL XII

Something unseen was moving in the black water beneath Flavia.

She panicked. Her body went rigid and her arms flailed. Black salty water filled her mouth as she sank down beneath the surface. She was drowning!

Then something strong and lithe and smooth pushed her up into the cool air and towards the beach. Flavia coughed out water and then filled her lungs with air. There was an odd wet sigh, and in the dim light of the green-gold phosphorescence, she saw a smiling face turn away.

It was a dolphin!

Flavia's toes touched softly corrugated sand. The dolphin had pushed her to shallow water. With her head and shoulders safely above the water, Flavia turned gasping to watch the others.

Three or four dolphins swam round her friends, describing luminescent loops and curves in the black water. Flavia could hear strange clicks and creaks and whistles: the dolphins were speaking to one another. They had their own language!

Her friends were laughing, and now Lupus – fearless as ever – clutched at a dolphin's dorsal fin as it swam past and managed to hold on. He whooped as it pulled him through the water.

Another dolphin was swimming in languid circles around Nubia and Jonathan, who were laughing and treading water.

Flavia felt a gentle nudge. A dolphin was beside her. Tentatively she reached out her hand and touched the dolphin's glistening back. It was like nothing she had ever felt: velvety but slippery at the same time. The dolphin circled and came close to her again, squeaking and smiling. Even in the dim starlight she could see that his dark eyes were full of intelligent humour. This time he tipped his dorsal fin towards her.

On impulse she grasped it as he passed.

Suddenly she was being pulled through the water towards Nubia and Jonathan. She squealed with delight as their startled faces sped past her. The water parted foamy green as her dolphin curved round and raced back towards the shore. Nubia whooped like Lupus.

Soon Nubia and Jonathan had found dolphin rides too, and all four of them were being pulled round the cove in phosphorescent trails.

Flavia didn't know how long they stayed in the water with the dolphins.

Once, she looked up and saw people standing on the shore watching, but they didn't seem important.

She didn't want to leave this vibrant, smiling creature so full of power and joy. Not yet.

Later, the four of them somehow found themselves splashing back up through the little waves onto the shore, where they were greeted with barking dogs and linen towels and questions. But they were all too exhausted to speak. Wrapped in their towels, Flavia and her friends trudged up the sandy beach to the villa, fell into their beds and were instantly asleep.

The next morning at lessons Jonathan felt deeply relaxed. For the first time since his return from Rome, he had slept soundly, without dreams.

Once or twice his father had treated him to a massage at the baths. Afterwards every muscle in his body had felt soft and loose. He felt like that now: refreshed and calm.

They had all slept late, rising when the sun was well above the horizon. His three friends had a kind of stillness about them, too. Lupus usually drummed on his thigh or his wax tablet and had to be told to stop fidgeting. But this morning he sat quietly. Flavia seemed calmer than usual and Nubia had a dreamy look in her amber eyes.

'Come on, you lot,' Aristo was pleading. 'We're diving for the treasure later and this calculation will help us determine the approximate depth of the wreck. Lupus. Do you know the answer?'

They were sitting at the table in the sea-view triclinium. It was another hot morning, with a soft haze over the calm, milky blue sea. Lupus was gazing out towards the horizon. Without looking at Aristo he shook his head.

'Jonathan,' said Aristo. 'How about you? Here. Take the abacus. Work it out.'

Jonathan took the abacus slowly. For the first time he noticed the weight of it. The polished acacia-wood beads on the copper wires looked like berries. Nutmeg-coloured fruit. A harvest of numbers. An autumn crop of sums.

'Jonathan!' Aristo passed his hand over his face. 'You're all even less focused than you were yesterday. What's got into you?'

'Dolphins,' said Pliny, coming into the bright room and pulling up a chair. 'They have a strangely calming effect on those who swim with them. Or so I'm told. Maybe this will interest you all.'

He carefully set a ceramic cup on the marble-topped table. Jonathan put down the abacus and leaned forward with interest, as did the others. The cup was a Greek kylix. Inside, the design showed a man holding a lyre and riding a dolphin.

'It's Arion!' cried Flavia.

'It is indeed,' said Pliny, and Aristo gave her a nod of approval.

'Please, Aristo,' said Nubia. 'Tell us story of Arion?'

Miriam had just come into the room.

'Your father's sleeping,' Miriam said to Flavia and then smiled at Aristo. 'Don't let me interrupt. Please tell your story.'

'Arion,' said Aristo, 'has always been special to me, because he was a lyre player from Corinth.'

'Just like you!' said Nubia. Aristo smiled and nodded. His skin was bronzed from their previous day in the sun and Nubia thought he looked very handsome in his fawn-coloured tunic.

Aristo cleared his throat and continued: 'Arion played the lyre so beautifully that Periander, the young king of Corinth, invited him to be court musician. The two men became close friends. They hunted together, dined together, played music together.'

'What instrument was the king playing?' asked Nubia.

'Um . . . Periander played the aulos, a wind instrument with reeds and two pipes. A very difficult instrument indeed, but one well worth learning. Periander was good, but Arion was better. In fact, he was the best musician in the world. It was said that if a man glanced at a girl while Arion was plucking his lyre then that man would fall in love with her instantly.'

Lupus barked with laughter, and when they looked at him curiously, he jerked his thumb towards the big bronze statue beside him. Medusa's already hideous face was shown contorted by a grimace of death.

'Well, it probably didn't work in every case,' admitted Aristo with a smile. 'But music is a powerful love potion.'

'Did it work the other way round?' asked Flavia. 'I mean, if Arion was playing and a girl looked at a man, would she fall in love with him?'

'Absolutely,' said Aristo. 'The only problem was that most girls looked at Arion when he played and so most of them fell in love with him!'

'Lucky Arion!' said Flavia.

'Not really,' sighed Aristo. 'He had lovesick girls following him everywhere. That was why he decided to leave Corinth for a while. He heard there was to be a musical contest in Sicily, with a fabulous prize for the winner. So he asked Periander's permission to go.

' "Absolutely not!" said Periander. "First, I have a bad feeling about your going; second, you might not win, and third, I'll miss you!" "But I'm a musician," said Arion. "I have the heart of a wanderer. Besides, if I win the prize I'll be rich and famous!" In the end he persuaded Periander to let him go.'

Aristo leaned back in his chair. A sea breeze ruffled his curly hair.

'He went, he played, he won. But on his way home, Arion discovered that the Corinthian sailors – men from his own town – were plotting to throw him overboard and steal his prize. "Take my gold," Arion pleaded, "but let me live!" "Absolutely not," said the wicked sailors. "First, you'll tell King Periander; second, he'll hunt us down; third, what good is gold if we live in fear for the rest of our lives?" "At least let me play my lyre one last time. After that, you can kill me." The sailors looked at one another and shrugged. They had never actually heard the greatest musician in the world play. "All right," they said.

'So Arion put on his best tunic, perfumed his long hair and went to the stern of the Corinthian ship. There he played the most joyful song he knew, hoping to change the sailors' hearts. But in vain. Their hearts were hardened by their lust for gold. The sailors approached him, brandishing sharp knives. With a prayer to Apollo and the sea-nymphs, and still holding his lyre, Arion jumped into the deep blue sea.'

Aristo picked up Pliny's cup from the table and tipped it so they could all see the image painted inside.

'Arion's beautiful music had not touched the sailors' hearts but it had attracted many creatures of the deep. As Arion sank beneath the waves, a friendly dolphin rose up with the musician on his back. The sailors were too busy counting their gold to notice.'

Lupus grunted his approval and Aristo smiled as he finished the story.

'And so Arion returned to Corinth, riding a dolphin

and playing his lyre. King Periander welcomed his friend with tears of joy, punished the wicked sailors and set up a bronze sculpture of Arion riding his dolphin. I have seen the sculpture with my own eyes,' added Aristo, putting the cup back on the marble-topped table. 'It's on the shore, at the very spot where the dolphin was said to have brought Arion safely home.'

After Aristo finished the story of Arion, everyone was quiet for a moment.

'Of course,' said Jonathan wistfully, 'nobody could actually *ride* a dolphin.'

'Why not?' said Aristo. 'You came close last night. And there are so many tales of shipwrecked sailors being carried to safety by dolphins that I think there must be some truth in the myth.'

Flavia looked at Pliny. 'Your uncle wrote about a dolphin who let men ride on it and then the governor wanted to honour it so he poured perfume on it but it made the dolphin sick. Where was that again?'

'In Hippo, on the coast of Africa,' said Pliny. 'What my uncle didn't put in his account, because he thought it too fanciful, was that the dolphin was friends with a particular young boy. He used to carry the boy back and forth across the lagoon so he could attend lessons. One day the boy caught a fever and died. The dolphin waited and waited and when he realised the boy wasn't coming back he purposely beached himself and died, too. They burned both bodies on the pyre.'

'Alas! That story is too sad.' Nubia's amber eyes filled with tears.

Lupus was writing on his wax tablet:

THAT CUP IS A BIT LIKE YOURS

He showed it to Flavia.

'Mine's older,' said Flavia. 'It's black-figure.'

'You have a black-figure kylix?' said young Pliny, his dark eyes widening with interest.

Flavia nodded. 'It shows Dionysus and the pirates, after he's changed them into dolphins.'

'By Hercules,' said Pliny. 'I'd give anything to see it. I collect Greek cups.'

'I have it here,' said Flavia brightly. 'I'll go and get it.'

As she ran out of the dining-room, Jonathan picked up Pliny's kylix. He held it carefully because he knew such things were worth a fortune. Only last month he had broken a Corinthian perfume flask.

His fingertips stroked the flat interior of the cup, smooth as silk where it was covered with black glaze, slightly rough where the shape of dolphin and rider let the orange-red clay show through.

Flavia came back into the triclinium and carefully placed her own kylix on the table.

'By all the gods!' breathed Pliny. 'It's the work of Exekias.'

'Who?' said Flavia.

'The most famous Greek vase painter of all.' Pliny turned the cup reverently in his hands. 'This is a masterpiece. Where did you get it?'

'Publius Pollius Felix gave it to me,' said Flavia, and Jonathan noticed she was blushing. 'It's my most precious possession.'

An hour later, when the day was hottest and the water calmest, the four friends and Phrixus made their way down to the beach. The dogs ran ahead, sniffing and watering as they went. Today was the day they hoped to recover the treasure.

Nubia glanced back at the villa. She could see several figures in the sea-view triclinium. Flavia's father sat propped up on a couch so that he could benefit from the sea breeze and enjoy the view. Pliny and Miriam and Aristo were also with him. Aristo had promised to catch up with them in a minute.

Nubia turned back and scanned the water. She hoped the dolphins would be there so she could swim with them again. Perhaps today one of them would let her ride his back.

But no fins broke the glittering expanse of water.

Nubia sighed. She felt strangely calm. The others seemed different too, especially Lupus. Something about his eyes had changed. They seemed softer, more open. For the first time since she had met him he had the eyes of a boy, not of a wary adult.

The dogs had run ahead to investigate an old fisherman who was pulling a battered yellow fishing boat up onto the beach beside their sky-blue one.

'Hello there!' The fisherman waved to them. He was short and stocky, his thin white hair a startling contrast to his chestnut brown skin. There were dark stains of octopus ink on his sun-bleached tunic.

As they drew nearer, he grinned, revealing several missing teeth. 'Want any fish for your kitchen today, Phrixus?' he called in a gravelly voice.

'What have you got, Robur?' said Phrixus. 'Anything special?'

'Yes, indeed.' The fisherman reached into the boat and held up a dripping basket. It was full of small silver fish, so fresh that some of them were still twitching. 'Look at these anchovies. There's a great shoal of them further out. Red mullet, too. And herring. I've never seen anything like it. Must be something to do with the volcano.'

'Did you see any dolphins out there?' asked Flavia.

Robur scowled and spat on the sand. 'Didn't see any,' he said. He lowered the basket of fish back into his boat. 'I hate the things. They eat all my fish. Especially my anchovies.' He caught sight of something in the boat and his face brightened. 'Have a look at this fine fellow.' He took an object from the boat and walked towards them, holding it out before him.

At first, Nubia thought it was a brown ball with pinkish-brown ribbons hanging from it. Then she looked closer. And recoiled.

She could see the round suckers on the octopus's tentacles and its human-looking eyes, frozen open in death.

Beside her, Lupus had been scratching Nipur's head. Now, as he stood upright, he stared directly into the blue eyes of the dead octopus.

Lupus opened his tongueless mouth. And screamed.

SCROLL XIII

As the inhuman scream died away, Jonathan turned and saw that Lupus was breathing in short, panting gasps.

'What is it, Lupus?' Jonathan knew what it was like to struggle for breath. He put his hand lightly on his friend's back and felt him trembling. But Lupus did not answer. He continued to stare straight ahead, unable to take his eyes off the dead creature in the fisherman's hand.

Instinctively Jonathan stepped between Lupus and the octopus.

As if a spell had been broken, Lupus turned and ran off up the beach. Scuto and the puppies bounded after him.

'I'm sorry,' the white-haired fisherman said to them. 'I didn't mean to frighten the poor lad.'

'Better get it out of sight,' said Phrixus quietly. 'Come on, Robur, show me what else you've got.' The two men stepped back to the yellow boat to inspect the rest of the catch.

When they were out of earshot, Jonathan turned to the girls.

'Did you see that?' he whispered. 'I've never seen Lupus frightened before!'

'I know,' said Flavia. 'He was almost . . . paralysed with fear.'

Nubia added, 'Like person when they see the head of Medusa.'

Flavia nodded. 'Yesterday in the library,' she said, 'I was looking through the ninth scroll of Pliny's *Natural History*. He says no sea creature is more savage than the octopus. It can grab a man with its suckers and then pull him apart.' She shuddered.

'But that octopus wasn't very big . . .' said Jonathan.

'And Lupus is seeing many terrible things,' added Nubia.

'You're right,' said Flavia slowly. 'Why should the sight of a dead octopus upset Lupus so much?'

'I have no idea,' said Jonathan. 'No idea at all.'

Lupus wiped his nose with the back of his hand and rubbed the tears from his cheeks. Then he stooped to pick up a large pebble. With an angry grunt, he hurled it into the water. The dogs thought it was a game and raced into the surf after it.

Lupus picked up another stone and threw it, and another. How could he avenge his father's death if he cried like a baby at the mere sight of a dead fish?

He shuddered at the memory which rose up before his eyes: an octopus lying in a pool of blood, staring at him with dead eyes. Eyes as dead as . . . No!

Lupus picked up another stone and hurled it. His right shoulder ached now, but he didn't mind the pain. Swimming with the dolphins had made him forget. He could not afford to forget. Not until he had revenge.

And to get revenge, he needed that treasure.

Followed by Scuto and the puppies, Lupus stalked back along the beach towards them. Nubia saw immediately that his eyes were hard again.

Lupus went straight to the sky-blue fishing boat and tried to push it into the water. Nubia and the others hurried to help him. The dogs scrambled in eagerly, before the ship's prow had even touched the water.

'Did I hear someone cry out?' asked Aristo, coming across the hot sand to help them launch the boat.

'Dead octopus. Gave Lupus a fright,' grunted Phrixus, as he put his shoulder to the skiff.

Nubia saw Lupus give Phrixus such a fierce glare that the freedman stopped pushing. But now the sky-blue fishing boat was afloat, bobbing on the water, gradually moving out with each small receding wave.

Phrixus pulled himself into the boat first, then Aristo, and they held out their hands to the others. Nubia chose Aristo's hand and let his strong arm lift her up and in. She smiled her thanks up at him, but his brown eyes were staring over her head, back towards the villa.

Lupus's heart had stopped pounding by the time they reached the site of the wreck. And his breathing had returned to normal. That was good. Nothing must break his concentration. As Phrixus released the iron anchor, Lupus stripped down to his loin cloth and tied the hemp cord around his chest under his arms. When he needed to surface, he would give three sharp tugs and Aristo would pull him up.

Lupus stepped over the side of the boat onto the new plank which Phrixus and Jonathan had fixed to the boat's hull. It seemed sturdy enough. He sat, legs dangling in the water. From here it was easy for him to bend over and scoop up handfuls of seawater. He wet the back of his neck, then his face, and took several short breaths.

Then he held out his hands. When Aristo had placed a flat, heavy rock in his open palms, Lupus filled his lungs one final time and slipped forward into the clear blue water.

The weight of the rock pulled him down and Lupus felt the sea close over his head and the weight of water above him, stuffing his ears and nose with pressure. A thousand silver bubbles peeled themselves away from him and rose up, as if he were a snake shedding his old skin. He opened his eyes to see a shoal of bright fish darting towards him, then veering away, as one.

It was nearly midday and the sun was almost directly overhead. At first, the water was bright and warm. But as he continued to sink the water grew cooler, darker, heavier. Presently, the water rushing past him was deep blue. And cold.

As he continued his downward plunge, Lupus tipped the flat rock so that it carried him closer to the wreck. He saw what he had not noticed the day before: the tattered remains of the ship's sail flapping in the underwater current.

As Lupus released the heavy weight-stone, he stopped sinking. Fighting his body's natural buoyancy, he kicked out and swam towards the wreck, a black shape against the blue water around it. The ship's front – its prow – had impaled itself in the sandy bottom. It was a merchant ship, like the one Flavia's father had owned, so there were no banks of oars, just the two steering paddles at the back. Above these, the figurehead tipped forward like a decapitated sentry about to topple onto the mast.

Another shoal of fish approached, gleaming like pewter in the murky light. They flickered away, each turning at precisely the same instant.

By the time he found the crack in her hull his lungs were ready to burst. He must get back up. Three sharp tugs on the cord around his chest.

As he rose up through the water, Lupus mentally marked the hull's breach in relation to the fluttering shreds of sail.

Don't breathe in yet, he told himself. Breathe out.

Breathe out bubbles.

Water warmer, lighter now.

There was his goal above him, the water's bright undulating skin, with the darker shape of the boat floating far above him. Still a long way away.

Must breathe. But not yet.

The water's increasing warmth and brightness told him just a little longer.

Must breathe, must breathe, must breathe.

Not yet, not yet, not yet.

NOW!

Lupus broke the surface of the water and sucked in air. As the roaring in his head grew quieter he heard his friends shout: 'One hundred and twenty-three!'

'Lupus,' cried Flavia. 'You stayed under twenty counts longer than yesterday!'

Lupus nodded, still gasping for breath. He felt dizzy. A few strokes took him within reach of them.

Hands lifted him into the boat, a towel enveloped him, dogs licked him and his friends patted him on the back. He waited until his teeth stopped chattering.

Then he took his wax tablet and – his hand still trembling from the effort of the dive – he wrote:

FOUND GAP AGAIN

NEED TO MAKE MORE DIVES

SCROLL XIV

Lupus knew what the others did not: you never made more than seven dives a day.

Six dives was enough to leave even the strongest man gasping like a fish on the bottom of the boat. Seven made your nose and ears begin to bleed, that was the warning sign. And after eight dives, maybe nine, the cramps gripped you, softly at first, then more fiercely, until the pain was excruciating and the only relief came with death.

On his first dive, he had found the hull's breach.

On his second he squeezed through the gap and into the dark belly of the ship. He realised now why no man had got inside the wreck before. The gap was very narrow, like a crack in a giant cup.

On his third dive, he found a great pile of amphoras filling the upended front of the hull. He pushed them aside, the round ones more easily than the long ones. But he found no casks or treasure-chests.

Back up in the sunlight, Lupus noticed blood on the towel. Not from his ears or nose, but from his hands, where he had pushed the amphoras aside. The barnacles and shells which had attached themselves to the rough clay were razor sharp.

He needed a break: to breathe and to think. The others were asking him questions, but he shut out their voices and concentrated on breathing slowly and deeply. Was there really gold in the wreck? There were no chests. No strongboxes. Only amphoras. Suddenly Lupus remembered the trick that Captain Geminus's patron had once used to hide some gold: he had poured the coins into amphoras, where nobody would think to look for them.

Lupus dived again, and on this – his fourth dive – he found some smaller amphoras. He knew the big ones usually contained grain or wine. If there was gold in some of the amphoras, it would be in smaller ones like these, because of the weight.

Lupus wasted his fifth dive trying to break one of the smaller amphoras. He needed to know what was inside. He didn't want to end up with a jar full of fish sauce, nutmegs or olives. None of those things were of use to him. Only gold could buy Gamala's swift cut to the base of the neck. He tried to smash one amphora with another, but the jars were well-made and the water made his movements too sluggish to be effective.

On his sixth dive, he was just feeling the urge to breathe when he found a small amphora with a broken neck. He needed to start back up soon. But first he would see what was inside.

Cautiously he lowered his hand into the jar. A shiver of pleasure ran through him as his hand grasped small, heavy discs. Lupus pulled out a fistful of what he had been praying for. Even in the deep blue gloom of the hull the glint of gold was unmistakable.

Stupid! Why hadn't he brought a pouch or bag? Every sponge-fisher knew to bring his sponge net. No time now. Desperate for air. Get it next dive.

He pushed through the breach and started up. He had never left it this late. But with his hands balled round the coins he couldn't tug his lifeline and he couldn't swim properly. He had to let the coins drop.

Lupus opened his hands and tugged his cord, then frantically began pulling the water to bring himself up. A shower of gold discs drifted past his kicking feet towards the sandy bottom.

But Lupus no longer cared. He had only one desire: to reach the surface and breathe.

Nubia wrapped the towel around Lupus and rubbed vigorously. His brown shoulders were shivering and his teeth chattering. Instinctively she felt something was wrong. He should be leaving himself more time to recover between dives. There was a strange, feverish look in his eyes. Now he was already pushing the towel away, looking for something in the bottom of the boat: his tablet pouch. He emptied out the wax tablets and tied it round his left wrist.

'Did you find the gold?' asked Flavia, her eyes gleaming.

Lupus nodded.

Suddenly Nubia uttered a cry of horror. A slow trickle of bright red blood was oozing from Lupus's left ear. As he turned to look at her she saw his nose was bleeding, too.

'Behold, the blood flows from your nose and ears!'

'Oh, Lupus!' cried Flavia, clapping her palms to her cheeks.

Lupus wiped his nose with his arm and saw the smear of blood there. He shrugged, stepped out onto the board, sat with his legs in the water and splashed his face. Nubia knew he was preparing to dive for the seventh time.

But before he could slip into the water again, strong arms lifted Lupus back into the boat. 'Oh no you don't,' said Aristo quietly. 'I grew up beside the sea and I'm no fool. There is no way I'm letting you dive again today.'

That afternoon at dinner Lupus sat sullenly at the table and refused to eat his food. Nubia decided he was still angry because Aristo had stopped him diving for the gold. She noticed that he kept staring at the statue against the wall, particularly at the Gorgon's agonised face, frozen horribly in the throes of death.

His mood affected everyone.

Finally Nubia had an idea. She knew drumming often brought Lupus a sort of peace.

'Shall we play music?' she suggested when the dessert course had been cleared away. If Lupus joined in he might feel better.

Aristo shot her a keen glance. 'Good idea,' he said and turned to their host. 'May we play?'

'Of course,' said Pliny. He clapped his hands. 'Phrixus! Bring our instruments, will you? And there's another lyre in the storeroom.'

Phrixus returned a few moments later and handed out the instruments. When Lupus refused to take his goatskin drum, Phrixus set it on the table beside him.

Nubia glanced at Aristo and mouthed 'Song of the Traveller'. It had a strong beat. Aristo nodded and began to play. Nubia sang, Jonathan thumbed the bass notes on his barbiton and Flavia jingled her tambourine.

Lupus ignored them.

When the song ended, Nubia looked at Aristo. He raised his eyebrows at her and she knew which song he wanted her to play: 'Slave Song'.

She nodded back and kept her eyes on him. They began together.

Presently Jonathan came in on the barbiton and then Flavia softly on tambourine, but the music longed for the drum. Nubia had to close her eyes to concentrate.

The first time she had played it, even though she

had played solo, the song had brought her a deep re-lease. She had known then that it was something special.

Later, when Aristo and her friends had learned to play the song, it had become something even more wonderful. But without the drum it sounded wrong.

Nubia felt a strange tightness in her throat. She tried to swallow but that didn't help, so she stopped playing and opened her eyes. Aristo stopped, too, and the song trailed off. He gave a small shake of his head and nodded towards Lupus's place at the table.

It was empty.

The slaves looked up with interest as Lupus entered the kitchen. It was a large, dim room with a vaulted ceiling and a coal hearth along one entire wall. The grey plaster walls were smoke-streaked and in places the brickwork showed through. Despite its drabness, the laughter of the kitchen slaves and the scent of dried herbs gave it a cheerful feel.

One of the figures detached himself from the group and came over. Lupus was surprised to see it was Phrixus.

'What is it, Lupus? What do you want? Buttermilk? Soup?'

Lupus shook his head. He had been expecting to mime his requests but Phrixus could read, so he unflipped his wax tablet and wrote:

BIG BEAKER OF WATER WITH SALT IN IT

In one corner of the kitchen was a stone sink full of water. Phrixus took a clay beaker from the shelf, filled it with water and handed it to Lupus. Then he passed the boy a ceramic bowl of grey salt with a bone spoon in it.

Lupus stirred three spoonfuls of salt into the water and drained the beaker.

'That will make you terribly thirsty,' said Phrixus.

Lupus nodded at him to say: Yes, I know.

Then he wrote a list on his wax tablet:

ALMONDS

DRIED FISH

OLIVE OIL

MORTARIUM

Phrixus raised an eyebrow when he saw the list and then called out: 'Rosa! Bring us some almonds, dried fish, and olive oil. Oh, and a mortar and pestle.'

A plump kitchen slave with red hair hurried to get the items. She dimpled prettily as she set them on the wooden table.

Lupus grunted his thanks and put a handful of

almonds in the large, flattish bowl. It was made of fired clay with bits of pottery grit embedded in it. Using a heavy marble pestle he ground the almonds to paste, then gradually began to add the dried fish.

Rosa and Phrixus watched with interest and soon the other slaves had gathered round. Lupus's forearm was already beginning to ache from the grinding. He switched to his left hand.

'What is he making?' asked Rosa.

'I can't wait to see,' said Phrixus.

When the fish and almonds were ground together, Lupus began to add olive oil.

Now his left arm was aching so he switched back to his right.

'Take over the grinding, would you, Rosa?' asked Phrixus with a smile.

The slave-girl took the pestle from Lupus. As he added the oil, she continued grinding. Her forearms were strong and muscular. Soon the mortarium was full of a viscous light-brown liquid.

'What on earth?' Phrixus asked Lupus.

Lupus sighed and picked up his wax tablet again.

SPECIAL MEAL FOR DIVERS he wrote.

Phrixus nodded, and then winced as Lupus poured the whole mixture into the empty water beaker and carefully tipped it down his throat.

Something woke Flavia from her dream of swimming with dolphins.

It was the deepest hour of the night. The ceiling above her was only just visible in the flickering light of a small clay night-lamp.

From across the room, Nubia's breathing was slow and steady. Everything else was silent.

Then Flavia felt it. Along the length of her back where it rested on the mattress. The merest trembling, first a purr, then a growl, then stillness again. Had she imagined it? She heard Nipur whine and felt Scuto's cold nose gently butt her hand.

No. She had not imagined it. The dogs had sensed it, too. She patted the bed beside her. 'Come on, boy,' she whispered. 'You can come up just this once.'

Scuto didn't need to be told twice. The narrow bed creaked as he lifted himself onto it, then turned in a circle to make a place. Flavia had to move right over until she was almost falling off but she didn't mind. She turned on her side, slipped her arm around Scuto's warm, woolly neck and gave him a reassuring squeeze.

Just as there had been tremors before the volcano erupted, this must have been one after. She wondered how much stronger it would have felt for those living near Vesuvius. And in Surrentum.

Presently she drifted back to sleep and into an

unsettling dream in which she was standing on Green Fountain Street in front of her house. She was locked out. When she stepped forward and banged the knocker, strange eyes appeared in the peephole: the brown eyes of a woman.

When Flavia awoke the next morning she had forgotten all about the tremor.

Aristo came into the triclinium as the slaves were serving breakfast. He sat heavily on one of the wrought-iron chairs and stared out through the pink spiral columns towards the sea.

Nubia looked up from her cheese and figs. 'Are you unhappy, Aristo?' she asked.

He turned back to the table and looked at the girls. 'Last night I had a bad dream,' he said. 'I can't remember what it was, but when I got up and opened my bedroom curtain the first thing I saw was a slave-girl crying.'

'And?' said Flavia, taking a sip of pomegranate juice.

'When I asked her what was wrong, she said she had been cleaning fish for supper this afternoon and she found one with no heart.'

Flavia slowly put down her cup.

'What does that mean?' asked Nubia.

'It's a bad omen,' said Aristo.

'Very bad,' said Flavia. 'The day Julius Caesar was

murdered, the soothsayers found the lamb had no heart.'

'And that's not quite all,' said Aristo. 'I asked her what sort of fish she had been gutting, and she said it was the fish called "lupus".'

SCROLL XV

'Maybe we shouldn't let Lupus dive today,' said Flavia to Aristo. 'If the omens are bad, he could be in danger.'

There was an angry grunt from behind them. Jonathan and Lupus had just come into the room. The younger boy had his hands on his hips and it was obvious from the scowl on his face that he had heard Flavia's last remark.

'She's right, Lupus,' said Aristo. 'You could be in danger.'

Lupus was already writing on his tablet. He strode forward and slammed it down on the marble table.

I DON'T BELIEVE IN OMENS

'Besides,' said Jonathan, 'I've invented a special float-rope that means Lupus will only have to make one more dive.'

'Really?' said Aristo. 'Show us.'

'Here are my plans,' said Jonathan, opening his wax

tablet and putting it on the table. He bent over and leaned his elbows on the cold marble.

'What's this line with little circles on it?' asked Flavia.

'That's my invention. I call it a float-rope. A few days ago I noticed about a dozen floats in the boathouse, for keeping the fishing nets from sinking.'

'I know what they look like,' said Flavia. She pressed her two fists together: 'They're about this big, round and light brown.'

'That's it. They're made of cork, a kind of bark. Well, yesterday, after we got back, Phrixus and I attached the cork floats to the end of a long rope. I used the abacus to calculate the depth of the wreck. I think it's about eighty feet deep. So I've made the float-rope a hundred feet, just in case my calculations are off.'

'Your calculations are excellent,' said Aristo, studying the figures on Jonathan's wax tablet.

'And Lupus and I have been doing a few tests in the heated swimming pool of the baths this morning,' said Jonathan, standing up straight. 'We tried pushing cork floats under the water. It's almost impossible to hold them down.'

Aristo frowned. 'If the floats are so buoyant, how will we get a dozen of them to a depth of eighty feet?'

'I've thought of that,' said Jonathan. 'The anchor is the only thing I could think of heavy enough to pull the float-rope down and keep it there. We attach the float-rope to the anchor with hemp cords. When Lupus cuts these cords the float rope will immediately rise to the surface, bringing the amphora with it.'

'Jonathan,' said Aristo, 'that's a brilliant invention.'

Jonathan flushed with pleasure. 'The most difficult part,' he said, 'will be for Lupus to get the gold-filled amphora to the float-rope, but the water should make it less heavy than if it were in the air. You taught us that.'

It was Aristo's turn to flush. 'You've actually applied something I taught you, Jonathan. That's the sign of a true engineer.'

'And look,' said Jonathan, 'Lupus drew me a picture of the amphora with the gold in it. The neck is broken but it still has one handle. So Phrixus and I attached this big fishhook to the float-rope. All Lupus has to do is slip the handle of the amphora over the hook. He doesn't have to tie a knot or anything.'

CAN WE TRY IT OUT? wrote Lupus on his wax tablet.

Aristo glanced out through the pink columns. 'Very well,' he said. 'Against my better judgment. But I want to wait an hour or so to see if that bank of clouds on the horizon is coming or going. Agreed?'

They all nodded.

'Get out your wax tablets,' Aristo said. 'Let's go over Jonathan's calculations.'

'Do we have to do sums, Aristo?' moaned Flavia. 'Couldn't you just tell us a quick story? Like yesterday?'

'Another story maybe of dolphins?' added Nubia.

'Well,' said Aristo with a slow smile, 'there is one more myth about dolphins. It's the story of Neptune and Amphitrite.'

'Neptune, the god of the sea, had a thick beard as green as kelp and swarming with sea creatures. Little scuttling crabs in particular.'

'Ewww!' said Flavia, and the others laughed.

'And as Flavia has just demonstrated,' continued Aristo, 'this seething green beard was not very attractive to females. So when Neptune fell in love with a beautiful sea-nymph named Amphitrite, she ran away from him. She did not want to kiss a man with a kelpy beard, even a god!'

Flavia and Nubia glanced at one another and Nubia giggled behind her hand.

'But Neptune was passionate about Amphitrite, so he devised a plan. He would win Amphitrite's heart by building her a palace made of pearls and coral and sea-gold. When it was finished, he told all the creatures of the sea to search the watery realms of his kingdom for Amphitrite, most beautiful of the nymphs.'

'What did she look like?' asked Nubia resting her elbow on the table and her chin in her hand.

'What did she . . . ? Oh. Well, let's see. She was very beautiful with a slender body as white as marble. Her eyes were violet, the colour of the sky at dusk.' Aristo had a dreamy look in his eyes. 'Her lips were pink as coral and her teeth as white as pearls. Her hair was beautiful: glossy, and thick, and curly . . .'

He trailed off as Miriam came quietly into the dining-room.

'You were describing her hair,' said Flavia, with a mischievous gleam in her eyes. 'Glossy and thick and curly . . .'

'And green!' said Aristo. 'Her hair was green.' He glanced over at Miriam, who was leaning on the parapet, and he coloured slightly. 'Anyway, Neptune loved Amphitrite and was so intent on having her as his wife that he offered a reward of immortality to whoever found her.'

'What's immorality?' asked Nubia.

'Er . . . immortality means you live forever, like the gods on Olympus.'

'Stop interrupting him,' said Jonathan mildly. 'I want to hear the rest of the story.'

'There's not much more to tell,' said Aristo. 'Delphinus the dolphin found Amphitrite hiding near the Atlas Mountains. He told her that she could live in a palace made of pearls and coral and sea-gold. If she came back. And he said that Neptune had promised not to kiss her too often. Amphitrite missed her sea-nymph friends and she liked the idea of living in her own palace. So she climbed onto Delphinus's smooth grey back and the faithful dolphin carried her home.'

'Someone else who rode a dolphin!' cried Flavia.

Aristo nodded. 'Neptune married Amphitrite and made her his queen. They were very happy together and had lots of little green-haired sea-nymphs. As for Delphinus, he was made Neptune's official messenger. But whenever he wasn't working, he was allowed to frolic in the foamy waves. And when, after a long and happy life, Delphinus the dolphin finally died, Neptune turned him into a constellation and set him in the sky, to comfort sailors at night.'

'The gods always do that,' said Jonathan. 'Same with Hercules. They promise you immortality and then they make you into a constellation: cold stars in the big black sky. That's not how I want to spend eternity.'

Miriam had been leaning on the marble parapet, gazing out over the water. Abruptly she turned to them with excitement in her violet eyes. 'The dolphins must have heard you talking about them,' she cried. 'They're back again!'

It wasn't until she was swimming towards the dolphins that Flavia realised someone was missing.

'Where's Lupus?' She stopped to tread water and look around.

'He's back on the beach, under the big parasol. With Aristo and the dogs.' Jonathan turned onto his back and floated for a moment. 'It looks like he's practising his breathing.'

'But why isn't he coming with us? He loved swimming with the dolphins!'

'Dolphins are making Lupus soft inside,' said Nubia, who had also stopped to float.

'I think Nubia's right,' said Jonathan. 'Lupus seemed different after we swam with the dolphins. It was the first time I've ever seen him sit still, without fidgeting.'

'Yes,' said Flavia, trying to float like the other two. 'And he didn't look as . . . tough as he usually does.'

'Then he saw octopus,' said Nubia. 'And the tough comes back.'

Jonathan nodded.

'Maybe,' said Flavia slowly, 'that's the way he wants to be. Maybe he doesn't *want* to be soft inside . . .'

Suddenly she squealed with delight. She had caught sight of four grey shapes speeding through the glassy water beneath them. One of them leapt high in the air and the three friends laughed as he splashed down again, drenching them with salty spray.

Lupus lowered his head and then lifted it again.

With red-rimmed eyes, he watched the dolphins pull his friends in joyous circles through the water.

One of the dolphins swam alone. Every so often it leapt high into the air and flipped, scattering drops of water like diamonds, then splashed back into the sea. Lupus knew the dolphin was trying to attract his attention.

Would it be so terrible if he forgot about his vow and ran down to the water to swim?

No. Swimming with the dolphins had made him feel soft. And weak. And if he grew weak he would not be able to avenge the murder of his parents.

Vengeance was his duty. His duty as a son.

Lupus sat up straighter and crossed his legs. Then he closed his eyes to the sight of his friends and their dolphins swimming in the glittering blue sea. He took several quick breaths. Finally he blew all the air from his chest and took a breath so big it made his ribs ache.

Then he began to count.

SCROLL XVI

'I think I had the same dolphin as before,' laughed Flavia. She spread her linen towel just outside the shade of Lupus's parasol so that the hot sun would dry her. 'I tried to ride my dolphin like Arion, but I kept slipping off.'

'My dolphin used his nose to pull me,' wheezed Jonathan as he flopped down in the shade beside Lupus. 'I was patting his nose like this and he started swimming and I was being pulled along and I was yelling stop, stop and then I was yelling no, don't stop!'

'And my dolphin is pushing my feet from underneath,' said Nubia.

'That was amazing!' said Flavia, unpinning her wet hair and attacking the tangles with a fine-toothed comb. 'Did you see it, Lupus?'

Lupus shook his head.

'When Nubia put her feet together and made her body stiff, her dolphin came from underneath and pushed her right up out of the water!'

Lupus nodded, but kept his eyes on the horizon.

Flavia stopped combing for a moment and glanced over at Aristo. He frowned and shook his head.

'So,' said Flavia, as she resumed combing her hair, 'it's turned out to be a beautiful day. The clouds are gone and the water's lovely. Are we going to try for the treasure again?'

Lupus sat on Jonathan's boat shelf and prepared himself.

He had wrapped a strip of clean linen around his ears so the water would not get in and make them bleed.

He had swallowed his diver's concoction earlier in the day and had also been drinking lots of fresh water after his morning beaker of salted water.

He could now hold his breath for a count of one hundred and eighty. Almost twice as long as two days ago.

He knew exactly where the small amphora of gold was. He'd been dreaming about it all night.

Jonathan's special float-rope was ready, attached to the anchor which would pull him down faster than any stone.

He had a sharp knife to cut the cords attaching the float-rope to the anchor, once he'd hooked the amphora onto it.

He even had a pouch which he could fill with gold, in case the amphora was still too heavy to lift.

Nothing could go wrong.

Lupus leaned forward on his bench and wet his face and then the back of his neck. After a moment he slipped into the water and swam to the anchor, which Phrixus had lowered just below the surface. Lupus checked that the float-rope was securely attached, then put his feet on either side of the V-shaped bottom of the anchor and gripped its T-shaped top.

Still holding this rough iron bar, Lupus took several short quick breaths until he felt almost dizzy. He forced the air from his lungs and breathed in as much as he could. Then he sucked in a bit more. And a bit more. When he felt his lungs would burst he nodded at Phrixus.

Phrixus tapped the wooden peg from the winch.

The anchor plunged down into the sea.

Lupus had never descended so quickly. The cold blue depths of the water swallowed him whole. He gripped the anchor tightly and closed his eyes for a moment. It felt as if his stomach had leapt into his throat.

He opened his eyes to see the wreck already rushing up to him. They had judged it well. He let go of the anchor and watched it continue its plunge to the sandy bottom.

His lungs did not feel like bursting any more. They felt good: full of air, and he had as yet not the least desire to breathe.

But as he swam towards the wreck he frowned. The gap in the ship's hull had changed shape and it was bigger. Much bigger. How could this have happened? Something was wrong.

Lupus easily swam through the breach. As he scanned the deep blue interior of the hull, he cursed inwardly.

All the amphoras had shifted position. It was as if Neptune had picked up the ship, given it a shake and put it down again. What could have caused this?

Lupus swam back and forth – touching, pushing, shoving the amphoras – until threads of blood drifted up from his fingertips. He searched desperately for the small amphora with the broken neck. Or even one like it. But the only amphoras he could see were almost as big as he was.

All his work for nothing! If only Aristo had let him make that last dive yesterday, at least he would have a pouch full of gold.

His heart was pounding now and he felt like howling with frustration. His anger had used up the last of his air. He must regain his calm. He would simply keep diving until he found the small amphora. Or one like it. But now he needed to get back to the surface.

He turned and kicked back towards the breach. But as he started to pull himself through the gap in the hull something in the black water stroked his ankle.

Was it seaweed? Rope?

The thing around his ankle tightened and as Lupus felt the grip of living flesh his stomach clenched. As soon as he turned his head, he saw its eyes gleaming in the shadows behind the amphoras.

Octopus! An enormous one! He clutched the rough timber on either side of the gap, tried to pull himself through to safety.

But the powerful tentacle was stronger than he was. Lupus felt his bleeding fingers begin to slip. Another moment and the octopus would pull him back into the dark belly of the wreck.

SCROLL XVII

'He's taking a long time,' said Flavia.

Jonathan tried to concentrate. He was counting for Lupus: '. . . one hundred and eighty-one, one hundred and eighty-two, one hundred and eighty-three . . .'

'I think I feel a tug,' said Aristo.

'Then pull him up!' cried Flavia.

Aristo shook his head. 'If I start pulling when he's still inside the ship, it could make him hit his head on the beams and knock him unconscious.'

As Lupus lost his hold on the wreck he thought quickly. If the octopus drew him deeper the other tentacles would grip him. Then he would be lost. Quickly he looped part of his hemp lifeline around a projecting timber of the hull. That would buy him a moment or two.

With the octopus pulling his leg and the lifeline cutting into his armpits, he reached for the razor-sharp knife at his belt. He knew from experience that he could not pull off an octopus's tentacle. The only way was to cut it cleanly. But to do that he would have to cut his lifeline first.

Part of his mind was screaming for air. But another part was calm. He had one chance.

Lupus fumbled for his knife and cut the lifeline. Then, as he felt himself being pulled deeper in, he twisted and hacked at the tentacle round his ankle.

The octopus reacted instinctively. A cloud of black ink mingled with its blood and even as the other arms writhed towards him out of the gloom, Lupus frog-kicked out through the gap.

He was desperate for air now. He couldn't inhale, but at least he could exhale. The bubbles rose and he followed them up, tugging at the water, kicking desperately with his legs. Up towards the light. But now, instead of growing lighter it seemed to be growing darker. And colder. He had lost his bearings. He slowed and stopped. Was he going up or down?

Lupus didn't know any more. There was no lifeline to guide him. He only knew one thing: that he had to breathe.

And so he did.

'Two hundred and ten!' yelled Jonathan, a look of alarm on his face.

'Pull, Aristo!' cried Flavia, and Nubia nodded.

'I think you're right,' said Aristo. He pulled the line. 'It's stuck . . . It's . . .' He tugged again. 'Now it seems to be coming up quite easily,' he said in surprise.

A few moments later they all stared in dismay at the hemp lifeline. There was nothing attached to its end.

As the water filled Lupus's lungs, a deep calm settled over him. He floated in a blue-green world, peacefully aware of the beauty around him. A shoal of golden fish flickered past him and then another, silver this time, like a ball of quicksilver that shifted and melted as it moved.

Lupus smiled. Something was coming towards him from the sapphire depths. The pale smiling face was strangely familiar. Lupus laughed as Neptune's messenger gently nudged him.

It was Delphinus, coming to take him home.

SCROLL XVIII

Flavia's eyes were red with weeping. Jonathan had his arm around her but his face was white as chalk. Nubia was dry-eyed. She sat stiff-backed in the boat and stared fixedly at the water.

At last Aristo surfaced and shook his head. He pulled himself dripping back into the boat.

As Phrixus tossed him a towel, Flavia burst into tears again. 'It's all my fault!' she sobbed. 'It was my idea to dive for sunken treasure. Oh Aristo! How will the gods ever forgive me?'

Aristo shook his head and pulled on his tunic.

Suddenly, a chattering laugh bubbled up from the water. Nubia rose slowly to her feet and Flavia looked up at her.

'Behold!' whispered Nubia. Then she burst into tears.

They all turned to see a sleek dolphin nudging Lupus's body towards the boat.

Jonathan took charge.

'Let me,' he said as they pulled the boy's dripping body into the boat. 'I know what to do.'

Aristo nodded and stepped back. They all watched as Jonathan knelt beside Lupus and tipped the boy's head back so that his tongueless mouth was open and his chin pointed to the sky.

Jonathan put his mouth over Lupus's and blew. Then he took his mouth away and pushed on Lupus's chest. Then he blew. Then he pushed. Then he blew.

After a while he looked up fiercely. 'Pray!' he commanded, and lowered his mouth to Lupus's again.

Presently some water gurgled out of the corner of Lupus's mouth. The boy shuddered, then coughed and was sick onto the folded canvas beneath him.

Jonathan sat back, trembling. Flavia hugged him and then hugged Lupus and then hugged Nubia and then hugged Jonathan again. Aristo wrapped Lupus in the towel and held him tightly.

After a time, Aristo passed Lupus back to the girls, who cradled the semi-conscious boy on their laps.

Aristo and Phrixus gripped the oars and pulled towards home.

The dogs stood at the prow, tails wagging, and Jonathan sat at the rudder, trying to steer through a blur of tears.

'Lupus almost died,' whispered Flavia to her friends, as they trudged across the hot sand. Aristo went before them, carrying Lupus up the beach towards the villa.

'He *did* die,' said Jonathan quietly. 'When I breathed my spirit into him his heart had stopped.'

'How did you know what to do?' asked Flavia. 'I mean, how to breathe some of your spirit into him?'

'I saw my father do it once. He saved a little boy. We were at some friends. Their three-year-old fell into the impluvium and drowned, but father brought him back to life.'

'Will it hurt you?' asked Nubia. 'Losing some of your spirit?'

'I don't think so,' said Jonathan. 'I ask God to breathe his spirit into me every day. That should fill up any gaps.'

'What do you think happened down there?' asked Flavia. 'Why didn't Lupus come up sooner?'

'Look at the marks on his leg,' grunted Aristo, over his shoulder. He stopped to let Phrixus open the villa gate and the three friends examined Lupus's legs.

'Behold!' cried Nubia. 'White circles on his leg!'

'Octopus?' said Flavia.

Aristo nodded grimly. 'And a big one, judging by the size of those marks.'

Lupus groaned.

'He must have been terrified down there,' murmured Jonathan.

Phrixus held the door open and they followed Aristo up the steps and into the hot, violet-scented terrace which led to the sea-view triclinium.

Still carrying Lupus, Aristo stepped into the bright dining-room.

Then he stopped dead in his tracks. Flavia and the others almost bumped into him. But they stopped, too, when they saw what Aristo was staring at.

Miriam and Pliny were standing close together by one of the pink spiral columns. She had her hands on his shoulders and she was kissing him.

SCROLL XIX

'Miriam!' cried Flavia. 'What are you doing? You're engaged to Uncle Gaius!'

Miriam whirled to face them and her cheeks flushed.

'I wasn't doing anything,' she stammered. 'I was just thanking Gaius for a gift.'

'Where's Gaius?' asked Jonathan, looking around.

'Gaius is my first name, too,' said Pliny, with a modest cough. 'And your sister is right. She didn't do anything wrong. She merely gave me a chaste kiss on the cheek.'

Pliny put his hand protectively on Miriam's shoulder, but it fell away as she stepped towards Aristo.

'What's wrong with Lupus?' she asked.

'He almost drowned,' said Aristo.

'Dear Lord,' whispered Miriam.

'Will he be all right?' asked Pliny.

Aristo gave him a curt nod.

'Jonathan saved his life,' said Flavia. 'He breathed some of his spirit into Lupus and brought him back from death!'

'Oh Jonathan!' Miriam ran to her younger brother and hugged him. 'I'm so proud of you.'

Lupus groaned and Aristo muttered, 'Boy's getting a bit heavy, here. Where shall I put him?'

'Put him in Captain Geminus's room,' said Miriam. 'There's an extra couch and I can tend them both. Follow me.'

'Lead on,' said Aristo through clenched teeth, and followed her out through the green marble columns.

'And suddenly Lupus coughed and was sick, and then he was alive again!'

Flavia was telling her father about Lupus's near-death experience. 'We think it must have been a giant octopus!' she whispered, with a glance towards Lupus's couch. Nubia stood near Flavia, who had perched on Captain Geminus's bed.

Flavia's father was propped up on half a dozen soft cushions. He smiled at the girls and closed his eyes for a moment.

Miriam had closed the latticework shutters against the late afternoon sun and the light spread a pattern of bright hexagons over his blanket.

'Is the sunshine in your eyes?' Flavia asked him.

Marcus opened his eyes again and shook his head. 'No. It's fine. It's a good room here. Very quiet and peaceful. And Miriam's a good nurse.'

Nubia looked over at the other couch. Miriam was

sitting beside Lupus and spooning chicken soup into his tongueless mouth. She was wearing a pink tunic with a pale green mantle wrapped round her slender waist. She had tied up her dark curls with a mint-green scarf. It covered the part of her scalp where some of her hair had been burnt away.

Lupus turned his head aside when he had eaten enough and closed his eyes. Miriam stood and put the half-empty soup-bowl on a bronze table beside his couch. Then she approached Captain Geminus and the girls.

Up close, Nubia could see Miriam's new earrings. They were fat little dolphins, with eyes like daisies.

'Are these the Pliny earrings?' whispered Nubia, touching one with her forefinger. It was heavy and she could tell it was made of pure gold. 'They are so beautiful.'

Miriam stood still and allowed the girls to examine them. 'He gave them to me because you all had your dolphins and he thought I would like some, too.'

'Why didn't you come down to the beach with us?' asked Flavia. 'You would have loved swimming with the dolphins.'

'I don't know how to swim,' said Miriam quietly. 'Besides, I'm looking after the invalid.'

'Don't call me that,' grumbled Flavia's father. 'You know I hate that word.'

Miriam laughed and showed her perfect white teeth.

Nubia sighed. Everything Miriam did, even her slightest gesture, was breathtaking. It was no wonder so many men were in love with her.

Suddenly Jonathan's head appeared in the doorway. He was breathing hard. 'Come quickly!' he gasped. 'You've got to see this. Aristo and Pliny are having a fight in the ball court!'

Built against the grain-tower between the garden and a colonnade was a sunny ball court. Flavia and her friends stopped in the deep shade of the colonnade and stared into the bright sunken courtyard. The ball court had smooth red plaster walls on three sides and a hard earth floor. Black lines were painted in various places on the walls and floor and Flavia knew they were markers for the ball, to tell whether it was in or out.

She had seen women playing the game once in the baths in Rome, and she knew that Aristo and Pliny were not doing it right. The ball and their wicker bats lay forgotten in one sunny corner and the two men were rolling on the floor.

At twenty-one, Aristo was older, stronger, and taller, but seventeen-year-old Pliny had obviously mastered some useful wrestling moves. He had his knee on Aristo's neck and was squashing the young Greek's face into the dirt. Flavia clapped her hand over her mouth.

'Admit it,' demanded Pliny, whose face was quite pink. He was twisting Aristo's arm back. 'You cheated!'

Aristo gasped and tried to speak. Pliny eased up a little.

'No!' spat out Aristo, and suddenly writhed under him. 'I did not cheat!'

After an undignified scuffle, the positions were reversed: Aristo, hair and tunic covered with dust, now gripped their host in a complicated twist of arms and legs. '*You* cheated!' He wrenched Pliny's arm. 'You're trying to buy her affection with gifts. Admit you love her.'

'Never!' gasped Pliny, and even though he was in the submissive position he cried, 'why don't *you* admit you love her!'

'Freely!' cried Aristo, throwing up his hands in a dramatic gesture and letting Pliny fall forward onto the hard earth. 'I admit I love her. I'm not a coward like you! I admit it for the world to hear. I love Miriam!'

Beside her column, Miriam uttered a choked cry.

Slowly, Aristo and Pliny turned their heads towards the shaded colonnade.

'Oh,' said Aristo with a sheepish grin. 'Hello, Miriam!'

SCROLL XX

'What,' said Miriam, 'are you two doing?'

Aristo had just helped Pliny up off the ground. Now he was attempting to brush some of the dust from his host's tunic.

'Um . . . We were just practising some wrestling moves,' he said. 'Pliny was showing me one called the Spartan Shoulder-pull.'

'He's a very quick learner,' said Pliny. He slapped Aristo's back in a gesture of manly affection, and the dust which puffed up started them both off coughing.

Miriam walked slowly down the steps and into the bright courtyard. She stopped in front of them.

'You weren't practising.' She looked from one to the other. 'You were fighting over me. Weren't you?'

Pliny dropped his head.

Aristo gazed straight back into her eyes. 'Yes.'

'I am not,' said Miriam coldly, 'some garland to be won in a wrestling match. I'm a woman. I'm betrothed to Gaius Flavius Geminus – or will be if he ever gets round to it – and I love him!'

'I'm very glad to hear that,' came a voice on the other side of the court.

'Uncle Gaius!' cried Flavia. All heads turned to look at the man who had stepped out from behind a mulberry tree.

Miriam turned to look up at him, too, a look of astonishment on her face.

Gaius smiled at her and opened his arms.

But instead of running into them, Miriam uttered a cry of disgust and rushed up the steps and into the shadowed corridor towards her room.

The girls found the curtain drawn across the doorway of Miriam's bedroom. Flavia scratched softly at the pale blue plaster on the wall outside.

'Go away, Gaius!' came Miriam's voice. 'I don't want to see you now.'

'It's us: Flavia and Nubia.'

There was a pause.

'Can we come in?'

Another pause. Then a very quiet: 'Yes.'

Miriam was standing by the window with her back to them.

'Miriam,' said Flavia softly. 'What's wrong?'

For a long moment Miriam was quiet. Then she turned around. Her eyes were full of tears.

'I miss Frustilla,' she said.

'Frustilla?' said Flavia.

'Old cook of Uncle Gaius,' whispered Nubia. 'Who died of fumes.'

'I know that,' Flavia said to Nubia. She turned back to Miriam: 'Why her? Why do you miss Frustilla?'

'Because she was so wise and kind. She told me all sorts of things that father never told me.' Miriam sat on her bed and stared down at her hands. 'Frustilla would have known what to do about all these men who want me.'

'But don't you like the attention?' said Flavia. She sat on one side of Miriam and Nubia on the other. 'You're so beautiful,' continued Flavia, 'I wish I were . . .'

'I *hate* being beautiful!' said Miriam, with such vehemence that Flavia recoiled. 'And don't envy me. You least of all, Flavia. Everyone loves you because of who you are. Not because of how you look. It's awful to have men stare at you as if they're starving and you're some tasty morsel of bread dipped in gravy . . .'

'I'm sorry, Miriam,' said Flavia. 'I didn't realise—'

'I hate them fighting over me when they don't even know me. They make me out to be some kind of goddess, when I'm only human. Frustilla knew that. She would have known what to do and . . . I miss her. I miss her so much.' Tears welled up in Miriam's eyes and spilled onto her cheeks.

Flavia started to say something but Nubia put her finger to her lips. Flavia nodded and put her arm around Miriam, whose whole body shuddered with sobs.

Presently, when Miriam's tears subsided, Nubia said, 'You are loving Gaius because part of him was Frustilla?'

Miriam raised her head and looked at Nubia with swollen eyes. 'I love him,' she sniffed. 'But I also loved Frustilla and the farm and the garden . . . I was happy there.'

Flavia passed Miriam her handkerchief. 'So it's harder to love him on his own? When he's poor and doesn't have Frustilla or the farm and the garden?'

Miriam looked at Flavia and bit her lip. After a moment she nodded. 'Is that wrong?' she said, and tears welled up in her eyes again.

'I don't know,' said Flavia. 'I only know Uncle Gaius loves you for who you are, not just what you look like.'

'I know,' said Miriam. 'But there are other things . . . There's your faith . . . his faith. It's so different from ours. He worships dozens of gods and ours is only one of them.'

Flavia didn't know what to say. So she put her arm around Miriam's shoulders again, and gave her a squeeze.

As she did so, she was almost certain she heard footsteps outside in the corridor. Footsteps going quietly away.

'Uncle Gaius, why did you come here? Is everything all right?'

Flavia's uncle turned from the parapet of the violet-scented terrace. His eyes were shadowed.

'No,' he said. 'Everything's not all right.' He looked at the three friends. 'Where's Lupus?'

'He's sleeping,' said Jonathan, coming out of the triclinium into the sunshine. 'He nearly drowned today. He'll be all right, but he needs to rest.'

'Poor boy.' Gaius shook his head. 'He's the reason I came. I need to talk to you. But not here. Somewhere private. And open. I need some air.'

'We can go into the big garden,' suggested Flavia.

Her uncle nodded, so Flavia led the way back through the triclinium, down another long terrace with the sea on their left and the baths on their right. The sun was low in the sky now and the mulberry and fig trees cast bluish shadows back across the bright green lawn and rosemary borders.

Near the centre of the garden stood an enormous and ancient mulberry tree whose trunk was encircled by a marble bench. Gaius made for this tree. He brushed some ripe mulberries from the marble seat and sat down on it. Flavia and Nubia sat on one side of him and Jonathan sat on the other.

Gaius pulled a scroll from his shoulder bag and turned to Jonathan. 'Bato the magistrate came to see your father yesterday,' he said. 'Apparently Lupus tried to hire an assassin a few days ago.'

'What?' they all cried.

Gaius nodded. 'A man named Gamala. He used to be a member of the *sicarii*, a group of Jewish assassins. Somehow Lupus found out and approached him in the baths a few days ago. He asked this Gamala how much he would charge to kill Venalicius. Luckily Gamala is a friend of Bato's. He played along: named some ridiculous amount which Lupus could never hope to raise . . .'

Flavia jumped up from the bench. 'But Uncle Gaius! He does hope to raise it. That must be why he wants the gold so badly. He wants to hire someone to kill Venalicius.'

'But why does Lupus hate Venalicius so much?' said Jonathan. 'I mean, we all hate him. But this is ridiculous!'

Suddenly Flavia knew. 'Venalicius must be the person who killed Lupus's parents and cut out his tongue!' she whispered.

Gaius nodded. 'Correct. It's all here.' He tapped the scroll.

'What is?' Flavia frowned and sat down again.

'The story of how Lupus lost his tongue,' said Gaius.

Flavia stared at him, then took the scroll and examined it. It was a slender roll of papyrus, without a central rod, sealed with a red disc of wax.

'Hey!' Jonathan exclaimed. 'That's my father's seal.'

Gaius nodded.

'Why is my father's seal on Lupus's story?'

'Venalicius must have told him,' cried Flavia, 'when they were imprisoned together.'

'Correct again,' said her uncle. 'Venalicius confessed everything to Mordecai. Jonathan's father swears that Venalicius has repented of his former ways. That he wants to make up for his bad deeds . . .'

'I don't believe it!' cried Flavia.

Jonathan frowned. 'Why didn't my father tell us this before?' he asked.

'Venalicius' change of heart is very recent, and this information about Lupus is very . . . private. I think Mordecai hoped that Lupus would tell you himself one day, in writing. But when we found out that Lupus tried to hire an assassin . . . that is very serious.'

'And dangerous,' added Jonathan.

'Exactly,' said Gaius. 'You've got to talk him out of it. Mordecai thought you might have a better chance of convincing him if you knew the whole story.'

'Do you know the whole story?' asked Flavia.

'I know enough,' said Gaius, getting to his feet. 'Mordecai told me the gist of it. But he thought you should hear a fuller account.'

He handed the scroll to Jonathan and looked up

into the fading sky of dusk. Above them a huge flock of starlings had begun to wheel and swoop.

'It's getting dark,' said Gaius. 'I have to get back to Ostia and return my horse to the stables. And I have an early morning meeting with Rufus and Dexter, the bankers.'

Have you found out any more about why they're trying to take our house?'

'Not yet,' said Gaius. 'Rufus has been in Rome on business. He only just got back. Good luck with Lupus. I hope you can help him.' He glanced towards the villa and for a moment Flavia thought he was going to say something else. But he only shook his head and strode towards a gap in the box hedge. Flavia and her friends followed him and waved as he rode off down the tree-lined drive. But he did not look back.

Jonathan sat back down on the marble bench between the girls. They all looked at the scroll in his hand.

'That's it,' whispered Flavia. 'The story of how Lupus lost his tongue.'

Jonathan nodded and took a deep breath. Then he put his thumb under the edge of the scroll and slid it up the textured papyrus towards the wax disc. He felt a pop as the seal broke. Slowly, the scroll unrolled itself in his lap. It was not a very long sheet, only about the length of his arm. He quickly scanned the text.

Flavia looked puzzled. 'Why are you starting at the end?'

'What? Oh, Hebrew is written right to left. We start our scrolls from the other end.'

Flavia peered over his shoulder. 'Your father wrote it in Hebrew? Why?'

Jonathan shrugged. 'I guess to make sure nobody else could read it, even if it was opened.' He frowned at the scroll. 'That's a strange rubric,' he said.

'What is a rude brick?' asked Nubia.

'The rubric is the heading. The title.' Jonathan pointed: 'Here. In red ink. It says *The Story of Philippos* . . . I don't understand that.'

'But you understand the Hebrew?' said Flavia.

'Of course.'

'Then read it, Jonathan. Please.'

Jonathan cleared his throat and began to read, translating from Hebrew to Latin as he went along.

SCROLL XXI

The Story of Philippos

My appreciation of beauty has been the greatest curse in my life. If only I had been born blind, like other people, I might have been happy.

Perhaps it was because my mother Elena was so beautiful. She was the most beautiful woman on the island of Symi.

Or perhaps it was because my father was so ugly. He was a sponge-diver with crooked teeth and small black eyes. His huge nose was a shapeless mass squashed across his face. Even from a very young age I couldn't bear to see them together.

Luckily my father was often away with the other men of the island, diving for the best sponges, so my mother and I spent many happy days together alone. I would sit and watch her weave and listen to her sing. Whenever my father came home, I ran out of the house onto the beach. When father sailed away again, I would return to my mother.

The summer I was seven, we barely saw my father. And it seemed to me that my mother grew even more beautiful. Her belly grew like a ripe fruit. Sometimes, when I rested my head on it, I felt something stir inside.

Then one day, my father returned.

He embraced my mother. Presently he saw me and lifted me up. 'How's little Philippos?' His breath stank of garlic and there were tiny black dots on the leathery skin of his nose and cheeks.

I thought he was horrible and shrank away. He laughed.

Suddenly my mother cried: 'The baby! It's time!'

Soon the house was full of women in black. My father and I were pushed outside. We sat beneath our grape arbour with the men from the village and listened to my mother's screams. At last she grew silent. The women brought out my baby brother and presented him to my father.

Then they told us that my mother was dead.

I hated my father. It was his fault she had died. The baby's, too. Sometimes I tried to smother it, but my father always caught me and beat me.

As my little brother Alexandros grew older, I realised that he had my mother's beauty. When people saw him, their eyes lit up. But their faces remained blank when they looked at me. Then one day I discovered the reason why. For the first time in my life I saw my own reflection.

I will never forget that day. I knelt over the puddle of rainwater for a long time, not believing what I saw.

I, Philippos – who was so aware of beauty – looked like my father. It was a cruel joke of the gods.

I hated myself and everyone around me. Perhaps my hatred made me even uglier. Gradually people had nothing to do with me at all. Only one person on the island befriended me. A little girl named Melissa, about my brother's age.

Because she was kind to me, I wanted to get her a gift. Something special. But the people of my island were so poor that we could not afford mirrors or silk or even the very sponges which we dived for. Then one day I found a bed of oysters. Although my father had made me dive the full seven dives that day, I decided to dive again. Diving was something I was good at. I would dive once more and get a pearl for Melissa.

I ignored the warning of the gods and made eight dives. Nine. Ten. I brought up oysters, but none of them had a pearl. Then my vision grew red: my left eye had filled with blood. The pain of losing the sight of one eye was terrible, but not as bad as the pain I felt when I ran to find my reflection in the water. A horrible monster glared back at me. A face that would make children cry and men turn away.

I was thirteen years old.

The injury meant I couldn't risk diving again. Now I was useless. Good for nothing. Melissa was still kind to me but I could see she was repelled by my blind eye. I decided to end my life and so I climbed a cliff above jagged rocks. But my courage failed me and I crept back down again.

Not long after that, my father sold me to slave-traders. He needed the money, he said.

On that day, I vowed revenge.

Twenty years later I returned to Symi, a rich man with my own ship.

But I had not forgotten my vow.

Unseen, we dropped anchor in a secluded cove and I went alone to my father's house on the beach. It was dusk. I hid behind a trellis twined with honeysuckle and waited for darkness, my knife in my hand.

It was not my father who came out of the house, however, but a beautiful woman. She had been a little girl the last time I saw her, but I knew it was Melissa.

Standing there behind the honeysuckle I prayed to Venus, vowing that if Melissa would have me, I would become the kindest of men and renounce my evil ways. I would stop dealing in slaves and use my money to help the poor and unlovely. Even as the thought occurred to me, I felt my spirit lift.

At that moment a young man and a little boy ran up from the beach. The boy sat down to eat and the man kissed Melissa.

As I recognised Melissa's husband, I felt something like a blow to my heart. It was my younger brother Alexandros. The gods on Olympus had played another cruel joke on me.

That night my brother and his son went fishing. When they were gone, I went into the house after Melissa. Vengeance was in my heart, but she turned away my wrath with kind words and we talked all night.

When her husband and son returned in the morning, something made Melissa scream. Before I could explain that I hadn't hurt her, Alexandros overpowered me and took my knife. I fought back and in the struggle he cut off my ear.

The searing pain drove me mad and gave me new strength. I won back the knife and used it. The boy threw himself at me, but I easily knocked him to the ground. Soon Alexandros lay on the floor, too. I stood panting, and stared down at my brother's dead body. There was no room for remorse now.

'If you ever tell anyone of this,' I warned Melissa through a screaming haze of pain, 'I'll kill you, too.'

'I won't tell,' she sobbed, but then my good ear heard a voice ring out:

'I'll tell on you! You're Uncle Philippos!'

My nephew must have been about five or six. A brave boy. But foolish.

'No, you won't tell,' I said. I took the knife and cut out his tongue before his mother's eyes. Then I said to her: 'I'm taking the boy with me. If anyone comes after me, he dies.'

SCROLL XXII

Jonathan stopped reading for a moment and swallowed hard.

'I feel sick,' whispered Flavia. The others nodded.

'I don't understand,' said Nubia presently. 'Who is Philippos?'

'Philippos,' began Flavia, but her voice caught. 'Philippos,' she attempted again, 'must be Venalicius' real name. He is Lupus's uncle. The one who killed Lupus's father.'

'And cut out Lupus's tongue,' said Jonathan.

Nubia was still frowning. 'This story is written by Venalicius?'

'In a way,' said Jonathan. 'I suppose my father wrote it down as Venalicius told it to him.'

'Is there any more?,' asked Flavia, swallowing again.

'A little,' said Jonathan. 'Listen.'

I left Melissa weeping and sailed away with my nephew. He was ill for many days but hatred made him strong and he recovered. When we docked in Ostia he escaped. I was almost sad. He had begun to remind me of myself at that age.

Flavia had been watching Jonathan's finger move from right to left as he read the story. When he stopped again, she pointed. 'What's that? Did you read that bit?'

'It's just another rubric. It says:

I, Mordecai, servant of the living God, wrote this story as it was told to me on the fifth day of Tishri in the first year of the Emperor Titus. I wrote it as accurately as I could and without making judgment. May God have mercy on my soul and on his.'

As Jonathan read these words a movement caught Flavia's eye.

'Lupus!'

The boy had stepped out from behind the mulberry tree. He was wearing a clean tunic and his arms hung loose beside him. In one hand he held a wax tablet.

'Lupus, we're sorry,' said Jonathan. 'We just wanted to help you.'

Flavia braced herself for Lupus's fury. But he did not run away or scream or tear up the scroll. Instead, he took a single step towards them.

'Are you angry that we read the scroll?' asked Nubia.

Lupus shook his head.

'Were you behind the tree the whole time Jonathan was reading?' whispered Flavia.

Lupus nodded. Flavia noticed one of his eyes was very bloodshot and swollen.

Jonathan pointed to the wax tablet in his hand.

'Talk to us,' he said.

Lupus stared down at the tablet. After a while he opened it and wrote:

HE TOLD ME HE KILLED MY MOTHER TOO

'Oh Lupus,' said Flavia, and knew instantly that she had made the mistake of letting him see the pity in her eyes.

He turned and fled out of the garden towards the beach.

Lupus stood on the beach and watched the blood-red sun sink into the sea.

Could his mother still be alive? Somewhere out there on a Greek island far away? He felt sick with hope.

Suddenly he saw something which almost made his knees collapse beneath him.

To the right of the setting sun was a huge black hole.

Part of the sky was missing. And part of the sea. It was as if the vista before him was a red and blue tent and someone had burned a hole in the cloth, revealing the darkness beyond.

Lupus closed his eyes for a moment, then opened them again.

The black hole in the fabric of the cosmos was still there; shifting and moving slightly, as if a wind from the void beyond was blowing through it.

In that instant, as he looked, Lupus remembered what he had seen when he had breathed under water.

The dolphin's smiling face had faded. The world around him had grown cold. Finally he had been surrounded by a terrible darkness.

Now his body was trembling uncontrollably and his teeth chattered. He could not take his eyes from the horror of the hole in the universe. Was it coming for him now? Maybe death could not be cheated. Maybe the hole would grow bigger and bigger until it swallowed him in its blackness.

As he stared, unable to turn his eyes away, the hole seemed to shift and grow lighter. Then he saw it for what it really was.

It was a huge flock of starlings, hundreds and hundreds, perhaps thousands of them, wheeling and turning in flight above the water.

Birds. Not death. The hole was only birds. His knees gave way and he sat heavily on the still-warm sand.

Lupus knew that this moment had changed his life forever.

Now he knew what Hades was like. And he knew

he should be there now. For the first time Lupus wondered how he had been brought back from death.

And why.

'I think I've solved the mystery,' said Flavia to the others. 'The mystery of why Rufus and Dexter are trying to take our house.'

'Go on,' said Jonathan.

It was almost dark. A thousand starlings had flown in from the sea in a long dark ribbon, and were now roosting. The great mulberry tree above them quivered with birds.

'This is what I think happened,' said Flavia. 'After we captured Venalicius in Surrentum, Felix must have sent him to Ostia to stand trial.'

'That makes sense,' said Jonathan.

'And we know that your father and Venalicius were in a cell together for over a week, and that they talked about very . . . personal things. I think that's when Venalicius realised how much the four of us had to do with his arrest.'

'My father wouldn't betray us!' cried Jonathan.

'Not on purpose. But remember what Uncle Gaius said? If your father believed that Venalicius wanted to become good, he might tell Venalicius about himself and about us.'

'I don't believe Venalicius wants to be good,' said Nubia fiercely.

'Me neither,' said Flavia. 'People don't just change like that.'

'Sometimes they do,' said Jonathan. 'I've seen it.'

Flavia shook her head. 'It's far more likely that Venalicius took advantage of your father by *pretending* to be good. That way he could find out more about us in order to get revenge. After your father was set free, I'll bet Venalicius bribed Rufus to help him seize my father's possessions.'

'Why?' said Jonathan. 'Why would Venalicius do that?'

'To get revenge on us,' said Flavia. 'And to get money. They could sell our house.'

'Or,' said Nubia, and clutched Flavia's hand, 'Venalicius could be living in your house himself!'

It was dark now but Lupus remained on the shore, sitting cross-legged in the sand. Stars began to prick the deep violet dusk in the west. Behind him lay a deeper darkness. Before him was the sea.

He wanted to weep, but he couldn't. Deep within, a small, cold voice was speaking to him. Revenge, it said. That is what you were brought back for.

Jonathan had always told Lupus that God spoke to him in a small voice, like a clear thought.

This was a very clear thought.

It spoke again: Revenge.

Lupus shivered.

Somewhere, out in the cove, he heard a deep sigh and a soft splash. Then a whistle. He knew it was his dolphin. Delphinus was calling to him.

Come and swim with me, the dolphin seemed to whistle. Forget the voice that said Revenge.

Come and play.

But the dolphin's call came from outside himself, and Jonathan always said God was within.

Lupus could not move. Presently he heard the dolphin's chattering laugh and a resounding splash. Delphinus had done one of his flips.

Lupus longed to swim with his dolphin and be free. But he also wanted to do what was right and avenge his father. He wanted to rid the world of a monster. If he didn't, who would?

Delphinus whistled again, plaintively. The whistle was fainter. He was swimming away.

Lupus got to his feet. Don't go, he wanted to cry out. Wait! But he couldn't call, because he had no tongue. He would never speak again. The reminder of what his enemy had done to him gave the voice inside him greater strength. Now it seemed to fill his head.

Revenge, the voice seemed to shout. Revenge.

And the other voice – the dolphin's – had gone.

The Ides of October dawned warm and soft, with a milky haze floating like a blanket on the water. It would be another hot still day. In the garden courtyard a slave was standing over a pile of burning leaves. Despite the pleasantly acrid scent, autumn had not yet arrived at Laurentum.

Jonathan turned from his bedroom door and looked down at Lupus, still fast asleep in his bed. He had not heard his friend come in the night before and had been hugely relieved to find him there in the light of dawn.

Tigris was curled up at the foot of the boy's bed. Lupus was curled up too, with his knees right under his chin, and even in sleep he seemed to frown.

Jonathan tried to imagine what it must have been like for Lupus to have witnessed the murder of his father at the age of six. Would he ever be free of that anger and pain?

Jonathan closed his eyes. 'Please, Lord,' he whispered. 'Please help him get better.'

Lupus's eyes opened, and Jonathan gasped.

'Lupus! Your eye! It's all red and swollen!' He was going to add, 'like Venalicius' in the story!' but he swallowed the words.

Lupus sat up in bed. He blinked and rubbed his swollen eye, then shrugged. He slipped on his sea-green tunic, laced up his sandals and pulled a comb through his tousled hair. Then he tied the strip of linen around his head, covering his ears. Without looking at Jonathan, he stood and walked out of the room.

'Lupus, wait!' Jonathan followed him. Tigris stretched and trotted after them.

'Lupus!' said Jonathan. 'We need to talk. I don't mean *talk* . . . I mean . . . you know what I mean. You have to forgive him, Lupus. Otherwise you're only hurting yourself. I know it doesn't make sense but I know what I'm talking about. Lupus! Wait up! Where are you going? What do you want in the kitchen? What are you –? Why are you grinding up that disgusting dried fish? Don't tell me you're still after the treasure? Lupus, you nearly got killed by a giant octopus and drowned yesterday. Please tell me you're not going to dive again today!'

'Good morning, pater,' said Flavia, coming into the dim bedroom with a cup of hot milk mixed with spiced wine. Scuto padded after her.

She put the steaming cup on her father's bedside table. 'I've brought you a breakfast poculum.'

'Flavia.' Captain Geminus stretched and pushed himself up on his cushions. 'Good morning, sweetheart.'

'How do you feel?'

'Better, thank you, my little owl.' He took the cup and sipped. 'Mmmm,' he said. 'Yes, I feel much better today.'

'You need a shave,' observed Flavia. She wandered over to the east-facing window and pushed the latticework shutter. Bright morning light flooded the room. The sun had been up for two hours.

'It's going to be another hot day,' she murmured sleepily. She had been awake long into the night, thinking about Lupus.

She turned and padded across the room, opened the larger west-facing window, and stretched.

Abruptly she stopped, her arms pointing stiffly towards the ceiling.

She had heard something. The wet clop of oars from across the water.

Carefully, she gripped the window ledge and leaned out, scanning the low fog which blanketed the water.

Suddenly a figure rose up from the mist, looked around, then sank down again.

'Someone's out there.' Flavia frowned.

'What?' said her father.

Flavia leaned out a little further and gasped.

To her extreme right a ship was moving slowly towards Ostia. Within moments, it would be out of sight. But now its sail was still visible above the blanket of fog. The sail was striped yellow and black, like the colouring of a wasp.

It was the slave-ship *Vespa*.

SCROLL XXIII

'Help!' cried Flavia, running down the corridor. 'Venalicius and his men are after the treasure!'

She collided with Nubia, rushing out of the sea-view dining-room.

'Venalicius!' gasped Nubia, pointing back the way she had come. 'Behold his ship is there.'

'I know!' said Flavia. 'And I just saw a man in a rowing boat right where the treasure is. The ship must have brought him.'

'What is it?' said Miriam, pushing aside her bed-room curtain.

'Venalicius!' cried Flavia. 'I think he's after the treasure!'

'But how?' cried Pliny, coming up behind Nubia. He held a small bunch of grapes. 'How could he possibly have known it was there?'

'What's all the noise about?' asked Aristo, coming out of his bedroom across the courtyard.

'We think Venalicius is after the treasure!' cried Flavia.

Aristo stepped through the columns. 'Where's Lupus?'

'I tried to stop him,' gasped Jonathan, running into the courtyard. 'But he wouldn't listen. He saw Venalicius' ship too, He's down on the beach. And he has his knife with him.'

Lupus ran onto the beach just in time to confirm that it was the sail of the slave-ship *Vespa* disappearing behind the promontory. His sharp eyes scanned the low-lying fog and he saw what Flavia had seen, a dim figure looking about, then disappearing into the blanket of mist.

A grim smile spread across his face.

This time he was ready. He had his knife, as well as his sling and a pouch with some stones in it.

If he got to Venalicius soon he wouldn't have to bother diving for the gold. He wouldn't need to pay an assassin; he could do the job himself.

There was a small rowing boat in the boathouse. He would have to take that unless – yes! The old fisherman's boat was there on the shore, and Robur was sitting beside it, his head bent over something.

'Morning, young lad!' Robur looked up from mending his net. 'Where are you off to in such a hurry?'

Lupus pointed out to sea and then pointed at Robur's boat and himself and back out to sea.

'You want me to take you out?'

Lupus nodded vigorously.

'But I've only just brought her in. Nothing much out there today. The fish aren't biting in this fog.'

Lupus flipped open his wax tablet and wrote

I'LL PAY YOU

He held up the tablet.

'Sorry,' said Robur. 'Can't read.'

Lupus rubbed his thumb against his fingertips to signify money.

'Want to hire me, do you?' Robur put the net aside. 'You don't look rich, but I suppose if you're one of Pliny's house-guests you can afford it. Twenty sestercii.'

Lupus didn't have time to bargain but he knew if he agreed straight off, the fisherman might think he didn't really have the money. So he shook his head and held up both hands.

'Ten sestercii? Don't make me laugh.' Robur stood up. 'Eighteen. I'll take you out for eighteen.'

Lupus knew he should have gone for twelve sestercii, but the others would be here any minute. He had to get to Venalicius before they stopped him. So he nodded and held out his hand.

Robur squinted suspiciously at him for a moment, then shrugged and grasped Lupus's hand in his leathery paw.

They shook on it.

'He didn't take the little rowing boat . . . it's still in the boathouse,' Jonathan was wheezing as he reached the others by the water's edge. The mist made his asthma worse.

'And the big boat is right here,' said Pliny. He squinted out to sea. 'Too misty. I still can't see anything . . .'

'Here!' cried Flavia. She had been walking up and down the shore with her head down. 'The sand's been scraped here as if someone just pushed a boat out.'

'Behold!' cried Nubia, who had been following her. 'Small bare footprints. Not yet rubbed out by the foamy waves!' The dogs bounded up to investigate.

'And big ones, too,' said Flavia. 'That fisherman we saw a few days ago, the one who frightened Lupus with his octopus . . . What was his name?'

'Robur,' gasped Jonathan, still breathless.

'I'll bet he's taken Lupus out in his boat!'

'Quickly, then,' cried Pliny. 'Let's get this one in the water. Aristo, will you help me row?'

'Of course.' Aristo already had his shoulder to the boat.

As the sun shone down on the sea, it began to burn away the mist. Lupus, leaning over the prow, was only vaguely aware of its warmth on his back.

Behind him, Robur stood at the stern, using the big paddle to move them forward. Lupus could hear the clop and drip as the fisherman twisted it in the water, but his whole being was intent on searching the wisps of shredded fog ahead. Presently the mist thinned and he dimly saw a boat with two figures sitting in it.

Lupus turned and indicated the boat to Robur, who nodded, his black eyes gleaming.

'Looks like Phrixus has decided to catch his own fish,' chuckled the old fisherman. 'Who's that with him?'

Lupus turned back and peered at the figures in the boat. Robur was right: one of them was Phrixus, holding a line of some sort. He had lifted his head now, had seen them, and the rising sun showed the look of surprise on his face. He turned to the person in the boat beside him: a man wearing black robes and a dark turban.

Lupus stared.

The man in the boat with Phrixus was Jonathan's father Mordecai.

As he continued to stare, a figure broke the surface of the water nearby. It lifted its head to speak to Mordecai and Phrixus, then saw the direction of their gaze and turned to look at the approaching fishing boat.

The man's head was wrapped in strips of white linen, but his horrible blind eye was unmistakable.

Lupus's jaw dropped.

Mordecai and Phrixus were helping Venalicius dive for the treasure!

'I heard something!' said Flavia.

'Me too,' said Pliny, and stopped rowing for a moment. 'Shhh, everyone!'

'Good thing we left the dogs on the beach with Miriam,' murmured Jonathan.

'Hear that?' said Aristo. 'We're on the right track.'

'The plop of oar in water,' whispered Nubia, and the others nodded.

Lupus watched Venalicius disappear beneath the surface. He was diving again. He was trying to get their treasure!

Grimly, Lupus turned to Robur and pointed to the anchor. It was a large iron one, shaped like the Greek letters *psi* and *tau* stuck together. He mimed hanging onto it.

It could only be dropped once, like yesterday. He would have to make this dive count.

'You want me to drop anchor with you on it?' said Robur in astonishment. Lupus nodded.

'All right, but I hope you know what you're doing . . .'

Lupus was already stripping off his tunic, strapping a belt around his waist. His knife hung from it, and a leather pouch. This time he would be prepared. He didn't need a lifeline.

'Lupus, wait!' Mordecai shouted across the water. 'He's helping us! Venalicius wants to help!'

'It's true!' yelled Phrixus.

Lupus started his breathing exercises, splashed water on his face and neck, ignored Mordecai's ridiculous cries as he climbed out onto the anchor. He gave Robur a nod, then took a final deep breath as the anchor fell away.

He plummeted down, and gooseflesh sprang up all over his skin. The water was colder in the middle of the morning, and darker. As the pressure mounted he was aware of his left eye throbbing.

Down he went, gripping the cold iron anchor, and finally he saw the wreck, a black shape speeding up to meet him. At the right moment he pushed away from the anchor and let it continue on down.

He kicked out towards the wreck and as he came closer he saw his uncle Philippos, also known as Venalicius the slave-dealer.

'Father!' cried Jonathan. 'What are you doing here? Where's Lupus?'

The three boats had converged above the wreck; Jonathan and his friends in the sky-blue fishing boat, Robur in his battered yellow craft, and Mordecai and Phrixus in a red rowing boat Jonathan had never seen before.

'Venalicius is trying to recover the treasure for Lupus!' called Mordecai.

'WHAT?' yelled Jonathan and Flavia together.

'It's true. I've been trying to tell Lupus.' The boat rocked slightly as Mordecai stood up in it. ' Venalicius came to the house yesterday and asked me to baptise him.'

'What is baptise?' asked Nubia.

'A kind of ritual to wash away your past,' Jonathan told the girls. He turned back to his father: 'Has Venalicius really converted?'

'Without a doubt,' cried Mordecai. 'Gaius told us Lupus was risking his life trying to recover some treasure and Venalicius offered to dive for it himself. To prove his remorse.'

'No!' cried Nubia. 'Venalicius is evil.'

'She's right!' called Flavia. 'It must be a trick!'

'You're all missing the point,' cried Jonathan. 'Even if Venalicius has turned good, Lupus doesn't know that. And he probably doesn't care. He has a knife and he intends to use it!'

Lupus did not need to use his knife.

Framed by the breach, Venalicius was writhing desperately in the grip of a giant octopus. As the slave-dealer struggled, his good eye spotted Lupus and he held out one arm in a gesture of supplication.

If he hadn't been underwater, Lupus would have

laughed out loud. Instead, he gave his enemy the rudest gesture he knew and started up for the surface. How fitting that Venalicius should be killed by his own greed.

As Lupus swam away from the struggling pair, something blocked his ascent. Lupus looked up. It was Delphinus, the dolphin who had saved his life. The whimsical face passed inches from his and Lupus felt velvet-smooth skin caress his shoulder.

He waited until Delphinus had passed, then kicked for the surface again, but with a powerful twist of his body the dolphin again blocked his way. This time the fish nudged him gently back down. Back towards the man still struggling in the grip of the octopus. The dolphin seemed to smile and Lupus saw the look of intelligence in its deep blue eye.

Delphinus didn't know Venalicius was evil. He only knew someone needed help, as Lupus himself had needed help the day before. Lupus shrugged at the dolphin, as if to say, what can I do?

Delphinus opened his mouth in a smile and even underwater, Lupus heard him click. A few silver bubbles rose from the dolphin's head. Delphinus swam towards Lupus again, tipping his dorsal fin as he passed. Instinctively, Lupus caught hold of it and felt a joyful surge as the dolphin pulled him strongly back down towards the wreck.

But then the joy faded and Lupus's stomach

clenched. Venalicius was still alive and writhing in the grip of the octopus.

Lupus wasn't sure which of the two monsters repelled him most.

Delphinus swam close to them. As he passed, Lupus let go and kicked towards Venalicius and the octopus. He still didn't know what he was going to do.

He pulled the knife from his belt and glanced back at Delphinus, who was making another pass. He heard the dolphin's echoed plea, sweet and mournful.

Lupus made his decision.

He steeled himself, for what he was about to do was repulsive. But it was the only way.

He swam forward and sank his blade deep in the brute's eye.

SCROLL XXIV

Phrixus started pulling. 'I just felt three tugs on Venalicius' lifeline!' he said.

'But where's Lupus?' cried Flavia.

They all leaned forward and fixed their eyes on the dripping rope as Phrixus pulled it faster and faster.

Suddenly two heads broke the surface, both clinging to the same lifeline.

'Lupus!' cheered Flavia and Nubia. 'You're alive!'

'Lupus!' cheered Jonathan. 'You didn't kill Venalicius!'

Venalicius the slave-dealer squirmed on the couch of the sea-view triclinium. Blood oozed from his nose and the bandage wrapped round his head had blossoming stains of red, too. The girls squealed with horror and Mordecai hovered with a moist sea-sponge.

'Dear God, what is it?' he muttered. 'What on earth is happening to him?' He tried to staunch the flow.

Lupus knew. He had once seen a sponge-diver writhe and bleed like this after his tenth dive. Shortly afterwards paralysis had set in and the man had died. Lupus clenched his jaw hard to stop himself smiling. He had only saved Venalicius to please Delphinus. Now he was glad to see his enemy dying in agony.

'Lupus.' It was Miriam, standing beside her father; she had been watching him. 'Do you know what's wrong?'

Lupus sighed and wrote something on his tablet:

HOW MANY DIVES?

Mordecai squinted at the tablet. 'How many dives did Venalicius make this morning?'

Lupus nodded.

'I don't remember exactly,' he said. 'Ten or twelve.'

Phrixus nodded. 'We couldn't find the exact place, because of the fog. And the water was still very dark,' he explained. 'It took him several dives just to find the wreck . . .'

Venalicius' body convulsed again and he stifled a scream. Lupus knew the pain would only get worse, and that it would only be relieved by death. There was nothing anyone could do.

Lupus looked at Mordecai and slowly shook his head.

'Lukos?' cried Venalicius. 'Where's Lukos?'

'Who's Lukos?' Flavia was biting her thumbnail and shivering. She had her other arm around Nubia.

Lupus stepped forward. Venalicius saw him and clutched Lupus's wrist.

'Lukos,' the dying man gasped. 'I'm sorry.' He writhed and tried not to cry out. 'So sorry for what I did to you and the others.'

Venalicius began to weep tears of blood.

Flavia screamed and buried her face in Nubia's shoulder.

Lupus shuddered with revulsion and looked up from the dying man's twisted face. At that moment, Mordecai moved aside to dip the sponge in a bowl.

And Lupus found himself gazing directly into the eyes of Venalicius as a young boy.

SCROLL XXV

Lupus stared over the writhing body of the slave-dealer into the face of Venalicius as a child. The boy was about his own age, with a swollen eye and a linen band round his head and an ugly face full of hatred. What was happening? Was the madness of the deep upon him too?

Then he saw what he was looking at.

Himself.

He was looking at his own face, perfectly reflected in the mirrored shield held by the statue of Perseus.

With a terrible clarity Lupus realised that he was becoming the person he hated most: Venalicius.

No one else saw what he saw.

Mordecai was sponging the slave-dealer's face and Miriam held the bowl. Flavia and Nubia were trying not to look. Jonathan, Aristo and Pliny were staring at the dying man in horrified fascination.

'Mother?' whispered Venalicius, looking up at Miriam. 'Mother? Is it you?' He tried to smile but only succeeded in contorting his face into a horrible grimace. Miriam glanced at her father and tried to smile down at the dying man.

'He's losing his sight,' whispered Mordecai.

'Lukos!' cried Venalicius suddenly. 'Where is my nephew?'

He tried to look round but his neck was paralysed. His good eye swivelled in its socket until it found Lupus.

'Please. Lukos. Forgive me?' The tears on Venalicius' cheek were no longer bloody, but the spark of life in his eye was fading fast.

Lupus did not feel the least desire to forgive. He was glad his uncle was dying. Perhaps if he refused the dying man's wish Venalicius would go to that place of utter darkness. That would be good. Lupus wanted Venalicius to suffer for eternity. He had saved Venalicius from the octopus. Surely that was enough.

He looked up again into the cold eyes of the boy reflected in the mirrored shield. His hatred made him like his enemy. And he did not want to become another Venalicius. That was too high a price to pay for revenge. He did not think his dead father or his living mother would want that.

'Forgive me, Lukos. Please.'

Lupus looked down at his hated enemy and gave a curt nod.

'Thank you.' Venalicius closed his eyes, smiling.

Suddenly Lupus felt a huge release. As if something

dark had pulled itself away from him and flown out between the spiral columns. And with the release came tears. Tears of relief, because his burden had been so great, and he was only a boy.

Venalicius was trying to speak but his paralysed lips barely moved. Lupus bent forward and his hot tears fell on the slave-dealer's face.

'Help . . .' said Venalicius, speaking in the language of his mother. 'Help the children . . . the ones I took.' And with his dying breath, still in Greek, Venalicius uttered one final word. To Lupus it sounded like:

'Rose.'

They burned his body the next day.

Gaius and Bato had travelled down from Ostia together. Mordecai pronounced Venalicius dead of natural causes and Bato made an official confirmation. The young magistrate offered to take the body away but Lupus held out his wax tablet.

HE WAS MY UNCLE

WE WILL PERFORM THE RITES

Pliny's slaves had already built the pyre on the shore and prepared the body. It lay in a litter on the terrace. Now four slaves dressed in black lifted it up.

In silence Lupus led the way across the terrace and

down through the gate towards the beach. It was a heavy, overcast day with a scent of rain in the air. A breeze ruffled the black garments of the slaves who carried the body. Behind them limped Captain Geminus, on his feet for the first time, steadying himself on his brother's arm. Mordecai and Miriam came next, followed by Nubia, Jonathan and Aristo. The dogs – including Gaius's huge hound Ferox – sensed the solemnity of the occasion and hardly wagged their tails at all.

As the procession slowly moved out of the triclinium, and Pliny moved to take up the rear, Flavia touched his arm.

'I have something to ask you,' she said.

He looked at her and then at the departing group.

'It will only take a moment,' said Flavia.

Pliny nodded.

Flavia held out the Dionysus kylix.

'How much will you give me for it?' she said, as calmly as she could.

Pliny slowly took the cup.

'Something like this,' he said, 'is impossible to value. It's worth whatever the buyer is willing to pay.' He caressed the cup with his fingertips and looked at her. 'Are you trying to raise a specific sum?' Even as he asked the question she saw understanding dawn on his face.

'Ah.' He tipped his head back and closed his eyes.

'One hundred thousand sestercii?' he asked without opening his eyes.

'Yes,' Flavia managed to say.

Pliny winced. His eyes were still closed. 'I haven't yet inherited my uncle's wealth. But I think I can raise that amount.' He took a deep breath and opened his eyes again. 'Very well, Flavia Gemina.'

Flavia exhaled with relief. When she thought she could speak with a steady voice she said,

'Can you find a way of paying my father's debts without him knowing it was me? If he knew, he would feel . . .' she couldn't think of the right words.

'Of course,' said Pliny. 'I understand. Bato and I will arrange it. We will be very discreet. No one else will know.'

'Thank you,' Flavia whispered and turned to follow the others. Quickly. So he wouldn't see the tears.

'Flavia.' He stopped her with a hand on her shoulder. 'You know I'll take very good care of this cup.'

'Yes,' said Flavia, without turning her head. 'I know.'

The body was burning fiercely when suddenly the heavens opened and the rain began to fall. It was a soft, autumn rain and they were not too wet by the time they ran back into the triclinium, shaking out their cloaks and brushing drops from their tunics.

Pliny's kitchen slaves had already laid out the funeral banquet. It was midday and the meal would serve as both breakfast and dinner. They settled down to the meal of cold ham, pickled fish and chickpea pancakes.

As usual, Nubia and her friends sat at the table. The dogs had all gathered underneath; they knew the best place for tasty morsels. The remaining seven adults reclined on the couches: Aristo and Bato on one couch, Miriam and her father on another, and Pliny flanked by the Geminus brothers on the central couch. The welcome rain had led to a discussion of the effect of the volcano on weather patterns and the Roman economy.

Nubia looked out through the pink columns at the pearly grey sky. She was not listening to the adults' conversation but to the music of the rain as it drummed on the parapet, dripped from the eaves and gurgled in the gutters. It seemed to be telling a story as it muttered rhythmically. If only she could understand its song.

She kneaded Ferox's warm neck with her toes, just the way he liked it, and heard him sigh with pleasure. Then she turned back to her cold ham.

'I've just had some very good news,' Bato was saying to Captain Geminus, who reclined beside him on the couch. 'An anonymous benefactor has promised to pay your debts in full. Your house is safe.'

Nubia frowned. 'What's an ominous –'

'It means someone has given him lots of money but we don't know who,' Jonathan whispered.

'Praise the gods,' whispered Flavia's father, and Nubia saw him drop his head to hide the emotion on his face. She wondered who had been so generous.

'It turns out Rufus and Dexter really needed the money,' said Gaius. 'One of their biggest loans was to a man who died in the eruption. He lost his entire estate as well as his family. They may not be good bankers, but at least they're not crooks.'

Bato sipped his wine. 'The volcano hit some people very hard.'

'It did indeed,' murmured Gaius, with a quick glance at Miriam, reclining beside her father.

There was a moment of silence and then Aristo said to Marcus, 'But it's wonderful news that the house is safe.'

'It's not all good news, I'm afraid,' said Gaius. 'I went to the slave sale in the forum yesterday. I'm afraid your brother was sold, Nubia. A representative from the school in Capua bought the whole lot for one hundred and fifty thousand sestercii.'

Nubia put down her pancake. She felt numb.

'What school in Capua?' said Jonathan.

Gaius looked at him. 'The gladiator school.'

Flavia said, 'Maybe we could buy him back . . . if we dive for that treasure and –'

'No!' cried Aristo, Pliny and Gaius together.

'No more diving for treasure!' said Flavia's father. 'It's too dangerous.'

And Pliny added, 'I think the gods have made it very clear that they don't want that wreck disturbed.'

'Besides,' said Jonathan, 'father says that if Lupus dives again soon he could lose the sight in his left eye.'

They all looked at Lupus, who put down his cup and looked back at them.

'Your eye looks a little better,' said Miriam. 'The swelling's going down.'

'No diving for a few months, though,' said Mordecai. 'Swimming is permitted. But no diving. Understood?'

Lupus nodded and resumed drinking the warmed poculum they had made specially for him.

'Also,' said Captain Geminus, 'it looks as if autumn has finally come. There'll be no diving or sailing now for several months.'

'That reminds me,' said Mordecai, lifting himself a little higher on one elbow. 'I have some very good news for Lupus. Before we left Ostia, Venalicius took me to the forum and we drew up a will in the presence of witnesses. I think he had a premonition of his death.'

They all looked at Mordecai. 'He left you everything, Lupus, including his ship. You are now the owner of the slave-ship *Vespa*.'

Lupus stared back at Mordecai.

'I guess Venalicius really did turn good in the end,' murmured Flavia.

'Told you so,' said Jonathan.

Nubia felt a strange tangle of emotions: anger, relief, confusion.

'You are not old enough to officially inherit yet,' Mordecai was telling Lupus, 'so the money has been left in trust to me, as your guardian, until you put on the toga virilus at sixteen. As for the *Vespa*, I will do whatever you like with it. Sell it, burn it, whatever.'

Nubia's heart was pounding. She looked at Lupus and he looked back at her.

After a moment he wrote something on his wax tablet.

Jonathan picked it up and read it out for all to hear:

I WOULD LIKE TO RENAME THE SHIP
AND LET FLAVIA'S FATHER USE IT FOR HIS
VOYAGES

Nubia felt a wave of relief wash over her. Yes. Let that ship which had caused so much misery be used for good.

Mordecai smiled. 'A wise decision,' he said. 'And as owner, half the profits will go to you. Is that correct, Marcus?'

But Flavia's father seemed unable to speak.

'Pater!' cried Flavia. 'Did you hear that? Lupus is going to let you sail his boat!'

'Yes,' said Captain Geminus at last. 'I heard.'

'By Hercules,' said Jonathan. 'You're rich, Lupus.'

'What will you be naming her?' asked Nubia quietly.

Lupus thought for a moment. Then he smiled.

DELPHINUS he wrote.

'You should really give a ship a girl's name,' said Flavia. 'Otherwise it's bad luck.'

Lupus pursed his lips. Then he used the flat end of his stylus to rub out and the sharp end to make a small change.

DELPHINA

They all laughed and Lupus added:

WE WILL CLEAN HER UP & GET A NEW SAIL
A WHITE ONE WITH A DOLPHIN ON IT

'I am glad,' said Nubia. 'I am hating that black and yellow one.'

SCROLL XXVI

The sun came out and glazed the wet columns and dripping roof-tiles with gold.

'Come on,' said Pliny. 'I have something I want to show you. All of you,' he added, looking at Miriam. 'It's not far, half a mile up the drive. We'll take the carruca.'

Pliny took the reins with Aristo on one side and Phrixus on the other. The rest of them squeezed onto the benches on either side. Ferox lay on the floor at his master's feet, and as Pliny flicked the reins and the horses moved off, Scuto and the puppies zigzagged behind the cart, sniffing the shrubs either side of the drive.

'All this land belongs to me now,' said Pliny, over his shoulder. He shifted the reins to his left hand and indicated with his right. 'It's mainly pasture for the sheep and cattle.'

He turned and pointed through the umbrella pines towards the sea. They could see the red rooftops of other villas.

'Most of that land belongs to my neighbours. But

here, where our drive meets the main road, we have a small plot of land and a lodge. My uncle tried to grow exotic vegetables and vines here once, when he was researching volume twelve of his *Natural History*.'

Pliny pulled the reins and the carruca rocked to a halt.

'Here we are,' he said. 'This little vineyard and those three olive trees belong to us. And there's the lodge.' He handed the reins to Phrixus, jumped down and walked round to the back of the carruca.

Scuto and the puppies were sniffing the dripping vines with great interest and Ferox joined them as Pliny helped the others out of the carriage.

Flavia could smell the musky scent of fox, and the rich aroma of damp earth. Somewhere in one of the olive trees a bird let forth a sweet trill. The early afternoon sun washed the wet vine leaves with liquid gold.

Flavia smiled at Pliny as he helped her down, then she took her father's arm, allowing him to lean on her. The boys ran ahead to explore the lodge and the rest of them strolled through the dripping vine rows after them.

Pliny fell into step beside Gaius, who walked ahead of Flavia and her father.

'The vines have gone a bit wild,' Pliny said. 'But at least they've been harvested.'

He stopped and uttered an oath. 'By Hercules!

Those peasant boys and their graffiti! What is today's youth coming to?' He glanced at Gaius and started walking again. 'As you can see, the lodge has suffered the lack of a tenant. But with a little work . . . and look! It has its own well.'

Jonathan and Lupus appeared between the two wooden columns of the small porch. 'It smells like something's died in here,' yelled Jonathan. 'We're trying to find the carcass!' They disappeared again.

Flavia's uncle Gaius stopped and fingered one of the grape leaves. 'They're getting the blight. You want to attend to this quickly, before it spreads.'

'No,' said Pliny, stopping and turning to Gaius. '*You* want to attend to it quickly.' He spread his hands, palms out. 'I need a tenant farmer and I think you would do very well. It needs a bit of work but I'm sure you're up to it. You and Miriam may have the lodge and land rent free. All I ask is that you give me half your output of wine each year. And that you invite me to the wedding.'

Gaius stared at him, then his face broke into a delighted smile.

Pliny smiled, too. 'Do you accept?'

'Oh Uncle Gaius!' cried Flavia, squeezing her father's arm in her excitement. 'Say "yes". You'd be so close to us and we could visit you and Miriam and it would be so wonderful.'

'Of course! I can't begin to . . . I mean –' Gaius

turned to Miriam and swallowed. 'Miriam, do you like it?' He gestured towards the lodge. Ferox had lowered himself into a patch of sunlight beside the well and was panting gently with his eyes half closed.

Miriam did not turn to look at the lodge. Her shining eyes had not left Gaius's face.

'Yes,' whispered Miriam, taking his hand in hers. 'I like it.'

Lupus had never written so much in his life.

When they had returned to Pliny's villa, he had gone into the library and found papyrus and ink. Now his hand ached and he was developing a callous on the ink-stained middle finger of his right hand. But he had finished. He had written it out. And it felt . . . not good. But better. Better to know his friends would finally know what had happened. He put the sheet of papyrus on the bedside table where Jonathan would be sure to see it. Then he walked down to the beach.

Maybe the dolphins would be there.

FATHER AND I HAD BEEN OUT NIGHT-FISH-ING. WE CAUGHT LOTS OF GOOD FISH AND ONE OCTOPUS. MOTHER HATED OCTOPUS. I USED TO TEASE HER. I COULD MAKE HER SCREAM BY HOLDING ONE UP WHEN SHE DIDN'T EXPECT IT. MAYBE FATHER DIDN'T KNOW THAT.

WHEN WE GOT BACK AT DAWN, FATHER WENT INSIDE AND MOTHER SCREAMED. I SAW THAT A MAN WAS THERE. HE AND FATHER WERE FIGHTING. THERE WAS A KNIFE IN THE MAN'S HAND BUT THEN FATHER TOOK IT AND PUSHED THE MAN AGAINST THE WALL. I KNEW HE WAS MY UNCLE PHILIPPOS THEY SOMETIMES TALKED ABOUT.

MY UNCLE SCREAMED AND GOT THE KNIFE BACK SO I JUMPED ON HIM. I TRIED TO PULL HIM AWAY BUT THEN I WAS ON THE FLOOR AND ALL I COULD SEE WAS THEIR FEET AND A DEAD OCTOPUS WAS LYING IN THE BLOOD STARING AT ME.

THE ROOM WAS ROCKING LIKE A BOAT. I FELT SICK. THEN FATHER WAS ON THE FLOOR TOO. HE WAS SO WHITE AND THERE WAS SO MUCH BLOOD AND I SAW MY FATHER'S EYES. THEY WERE DEAD LIKE THE OCTOPUS.

I HEARD A VOICE SCREAMING YOU KILLED HIM YOU KILLED MY FATHER! I'LL TELL ON YOU! IT WAS ME. THE VOICE WAS ME.

MY UNCLE TURNED AND CAME TOWARDS ME. HE HAD THE KNIFE IN HIS HAND. I DON'T REMEMBER WHAT HAPPENED NEXT.

LATER IN THE BOAT SOME SAILORS SAID
THAT I WOULD DIE IF THEY DIDN'T STOP
THE BLEEDING. DO YOU WANT TO LIVE
THEY ASKED ME. I NODDED. I WANTED TO
LIVE SO I COULD KILL MY UNCLE.

YOU HAVE TO BE BRAVE SAID THE SAILOR.
BRAVER THAN YOU'VE EVER BEEN IN YOUR
LIFE. THIS SPOON IS RED HOT FROM THE
COALS, SAID THE SAILOR. I HAVE TO PUSH IT
AGAINST THE PLACE WHERE YOUR TONGUE
HAS BEEN CUT OUT. THE ONLY WAY I CAN
DO THAT IS IF YOU OPEN YOUR MOUTH AND
LET ME. DO YOU UNDERSTAND?

SO I OPENED MY MOUTH BECAUSE I
THOUGHT IT COULDN'T HURT ANY MORE
THAN IT ALREADY DID BUT I WAS WRONG.

Nubia stood by the parapet and gazed out over the
water as Mordecai read the message Jonathan had
found by his bed.

'I think it's good he shared this with you,' said
Mordecai, as he finished. 'It means the healing can
begin.'

'Incredible to think what he's been through,' said
Aristo quietly. 'How he lost his family.'

'We're his family now,' said Flavia firmly. 'And now
that he has his own ship we can go and rescue all the

children that Venalicius captured. Rose and the others. Can't we, pater?'

Marcus gave her a weak smile. 'Lupus is the owner now. He can do what he likes.'

'I think Lupus will be all right,' said Jonathan.

'I think Lupus will be very all right,' said Nubia from the parapet. 'Behold!'

They all moved to the marble half-wall and gazed out over the blue Tyrrhenian Sea.

Far out in the water, silhouetted against the setting sun, they saw a sight none of them would ever forget.

It was a boy riding a dolphin.

FINIS

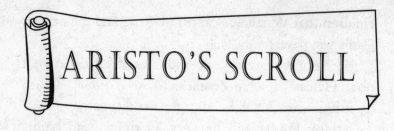

ARISTO'S SCROLL

Amphitrite (am-fee-*try*-tee)
beautiful sea-nymph (minor goddess) loved by Neptune, god of the sea

amphora (am-*for*-a)
large clay storage jar for holding wine, oil or grain

Arion (*air*-ee-uhn)
mythical musician from Corinth who rode on the back of a dolphin

atrium (*eh*-tree-um)
the reception room in larger Roman homes, often with skylight and pool

aulos (*owl*-oss)
a wind instrument with double pipes; reeds probably gave it a buzzy sound

barbiton (*bar*-bi-ton)
a kind of Greek bass lyre; NB: there is no evidence for a 'Syrian barbiton'

basilica (buh-*sill*-ik-uh)
Roman building in the forum which housed law courts, offices and cells

Capua (*cap*-yoo-uh)
a town south of Rome famed for its gladiator school

carruca (kuh-*roo*-kuh)

a four-wheeled travelling coach, often covered

Charybdis (kar-*ib*-diss)

a mythical whirlpool near Sicily that could destroy
entire ships

cicada (sick-*ah*-duh)

an insect like a grasshopper that chirrs during the day

Cicero (*siss*-er-oh)

Rome's greatest orator; lived from 106–43 BC

Corinth (*kor*-inth)

Greek port town with a large Jewish population

Delphinus (dell-*fee*-nuss)

the Latin word for dolphin; a constellation of the same
name

Dionysus (die-oh-*nye*-suss)

Greek god of vineyards and wine

dithyramb (*dith*-i-ram)

a kind of Greek hymn or poem, often passionate and wild

Fortuna (for-*tew*-nuh)

the goddess of good luck and success

forum (*for*-um)

ancient marketplace and civic centre in Roman towns

freedman (*freed*-man)

a slave who has been granted freedom

Hebrew (*hee*-brew)

holy language of the Bible, spoken by (religious) Jews in
the first century

Herculaneum (herk-you-*lane*-ee-um)

town at the foot of Vesuvius, buried by the eruption in
August AD 79

Ides (eyedz)

the 13th day of most months in the Roman calendar, but
the 15th in March, May, July and October

impluvium (im-*ploo*-vee-um)

a rainwater pool under a skylight in the atrium

Judaea (jew-*dee*-ah)

ancient province of the Roman Empire; modern Israel

Juno (*jew*-no)

queen of the Roman gods and wife of the god Jupiter

krater (*kra*-tare)

big Greek ceramic bowl for mixing wine, often beautifully decorated

kylix (*kye*-licks)

elegant Greek wine cup, especially for dinner parties

Laurentum (lore-*ent*-um)

village on the coast of Italy a few miles south of Ostia

Livy (*liv*-ee)

famous Roman historian, lived from 59 BC–AD 12

Meditrinalia (med-i-trin-*all*-ya)

Roman festival celebrating the wine harvest

Medusa (m-*dyoo*-suh)

hideous female monster with snaky hair and a face so
ugly it turned men to stone

Misenum (my-*see*-num)

Ancient Rome's chief naval harbour, near Naples

mortarium (more-*tar*-ee-um)

rought flat pottery bowl, embedded with grit, for grinding spices, etc.

Odysseus (oh-*diss*-yooss)

Greek hero who fought against Troy; his journey home took ten years

Ostia (*oss*-tee-ah)

the port of ancient Rome and home town of Flavia Gemina

palaestra (pal-*eye*-struh)

the (usually open air) exercise area of public baths

papyrus (puh-*pie*-russ)

cheap writing material, made of Egyptian reeds

Periander (*pair*-ee-an-der)

mythological King of Corinth

peristyle (*pair*-ee-style)

a columned walkway around an inner garden or court-yard

Perseus (*purr*-syooss)

mythological son of Jupiter and Danae, his task was to get Medusa's head

Pliny (*plin*-ee)

(the Elder) famous Roman author; died in the AD 79 eruption of Vesuvius

Pliny (*plin*-ee)

(the Younger) nephew of Pliny the Elder; became famous for his letters

poculum (*pock*-you-lum)

a cup or the drink inside the cup; in this story a mixture of spiced wine and milk

Pompeii (pom-*pay*)

a prosperous coastal town buried by the eruption of Vesuvius in AD 79

scroll (skrole)

a papyrus or parchment 'book', unrolled from side to side as it was read

Scylla (*skill*-uh)

a mythical sea-monster whose seven heads devoured passing sailors

sestercii (sess-*tur*-see)

more than one sestercius, a silver coin

sica (*sick*-ah)

small sickle-shaped dagger used by Jewish assassins (*sicarii*) in the 1st century AD

Stabia (sta-*bee*-ah)

modern Castellammare di Stabia; a town south of Pompeii

stylus (*stile*-uss)

a metal, wood or ivory tool for writing on wax tablets

Surrentum (sir-*wren*-tum)

modern Sorrento, a pretty harbour town south of Vesuvius

Symi (*sim*-ee)

Greek island near Rhodes, famous in antiquity for its sponge fishing industry

Thetis (*thet*-iss)

   beautiful sea-nymph; mother of the Greek hero Achilles

Tishri (*tish*-ree)

   the month of the Jewish calendar roughly corresponding to September/October

Titus (*tie*-tuss)

   Emperor of Rome and son of Vespasian, aged 39 when this story takes place; (full name: Titus Flavius Vespasianus)

toga (*toe*-ga)

   a blanket-like outer garment, worn by freeborn men and boys

triclinium (tri-*clin*-ee-um)

   ancient Roman dining-room, usually with three couches to recline on

tunic (*tew*-nic)

   a piece of clothing like a big T-shirt; children often wore a long-sleeved one

Tyrrhenian (tur-*wren*-ee-un)

   the name of the sea off the coast of Ostia and Laurentum

Vesuvius (vuh-*soo*-vee-yus)

   the volcano near Naples which first erupted on 24 August AD 79

wax tablet

   a wax-covered rectangle of wood used for making notes

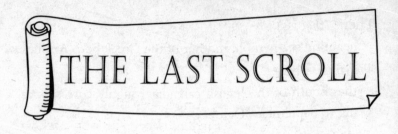

THE LAST SCROLL

Pliny the Younger is the only real person in this story. He was Admiral Pliny's nephew, aged seventeen when he witnessed the eruption of Vesuvius in AD 79. Many years later he wrote about the eruption in a letter to the Roman historian Tacitus. Pliny the Younger is famous today because of the letters he wrote. He published most of them in his lifetime, hoping that they might bring him lasting fame. He got his wish.

In another of his letters, Pliny the Younger describes his beautiful seaside villa on the coast at Laurentum near Ostia. His description is so captivating that many people over the centuries have tried to find or recreate Pliny's 'Laurentine villa'. There is a site a few miles south of Ostia called Villa di Plinio, but scholars are not sure whether this was really Pliny's villa or not.

My plan at the front of this book is based on many ~~s~~peculative plans and on the seventeenth letter in ~~Pliny'~~s second scroll.

~~In anci~~ent times, sponge-divers were often crippled ~~and deafene~~d by their profession.

CAROLINE LAWRENCE

Caroline Lawrence is American. She grew up in California and came to England when she won a scholarship to Cambridge to study Classical Archaeology. She lives by the river in London with her husband, a writer and graphic designer. In 2009, Caroline was awarded the Classics Association Prize for 'a significant contribution to the public understanding of Classics'.

She also writes *The Roman Mystery Scrolls* – a hilarious and action-packed series of shorter mysteries featuring Threptus, a former beggar boy turned apprentice to a Roman soothsayer.

And don't miss Caroline's whip-cracking new series, *The P.K. Pinkerton Mysteries*, set in America's Wild West and starring Virginia City's newest detective, P.K. Pinkerton, as he fights crime against a backdrop of gamblers, gun-slingers and deadly desperados!

Choose one of the twin portals on Caroline's website www.carolinelawrence.com to enter
Ancient Rome www.romanmysteries.com
The Wild West www.pkpinkerton.com